"I have absolutely no intention of making love to you."

"Good, because I have no intention of making love to you, either," Natalie said.

Jonah's kiss came hard and fast, and she moaned with delight. Pushing her down against the leather bench, he began working at the buttons of her blouse as he continued to kiss her.

She pulled his knit shirt from the waistband of his slacks and ran her hands up underneath to feel the play of muscles across his broad back. To touch him was heaven. To be touched by him was...unbelievable. She gasped as he unfastened her bra and cupped her breast. It was the right touch, the one she'd waited for, dreamed of... She saw stars. She heard bells.

Or rather one bell, which was ringing rather persistently.

He lifted his mouth from hers. "Lunch," he said raggedly. "If we..." He paused to take a deep breath. "If we don't go on deck, they're liable to come down after us."

"Oh," she whispered. "I'd forgotten about the media circus surrounding this date. Do you think the TV crews are still out there?"

"It's very likely," Jonah answered. "And unless you want the world to know that you *haven't* been making love with your $33,000 man, I'd suggest we get dressed."

Dear Reader,

In 1999, Harlequin will celebrate its 50th anniversary in North America. Canadian publishing executive Richard Bonnycastle founded the company in 1949. Back then, they published a wide variety of American and British paperbacks—from mysteries and Westerns, to classics and cookbooks. In later years, the company focused on romance exclusively, and today Harlequin is the world's leading publisher of series romance fiction. Our books are sold in over one hundred countries and published in more than twenty-three languages. Love stories are a universal experience!

Harlequin Temptation is delighted to help celebrate this very special anniversary. We're throwing a bachelor auction...and you're invited! Join five of our leading authors as they put a sexy hero on the auction block. Sparks fly when the heroines get a chance to bid on their fantasy men.

Bestselling author Vicki Lewis Thompson has created a delightful story about a bashful hero who's very uncomfortable in the limelight, but not in the heroine's bed, in *Single, Sexy...and Sold!*, the second book in this exciting miniseries. Vicki is truly one of Harlequin's stars. She's been with Temptation since the series' launch fifteen years ago, and has almost fifty books to her credit. Be sure to watch for her upcoming romantic comedy, *With a Stetson and a Smile,* available in May in Harlequin's newest series, Duets.

Each month, we strive to bring you the very best stories and writers. And we plan to keep doing that for the next fifty years!

Happy Anniversary,

Birgit Davis-Todd
Senior Editor
Harlequin Temptation

Vicki Lewis Thompson
SINGLE, SEXY...
AND SOLD!

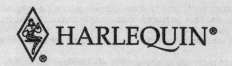

HARLEQUIN®

TORONTO • NEW YORK • LONDON
AMSTERDAM • PARIS • SYDNEY • HAMBURG
STOCKHOLM • ATHENS • TOKYO • MILAN • MADRID
PRAGUE • WARSAW • BUDAPEST • AUCKLAND

For Audrey and Dan,
who will live happily ever after.

ISBN 0-373-25821-6

SINGLE, SEXY...AND SOLD!

Prologue

THE PUPPY HADN'T worked out, either.

Natalie's breath frosted the air as she stood beside the lake in Central Park and played out the leash while Bobo searched for the perfect place to squat. Not far away a camera crew from WOR-TV was taking scenic shots, probably to use on the evening weather report. Natalie watched them for a minute before returning her attention to the puppy.

Damn, he was cute—jet-black except for a white spot on his tummy where he loved to be scratched. She'd been sure his floppy ears, stubby legs and soulful eyes would captivate her mother. But Bobo hadn't rated any more attention than the herb garden, the laptop computer, the aromatherapy unit or the home gym Natalie had hauled up to her mother's apartment. Six months after her husband's death, Alice LeBlanc did nothing but work thousand-piece jigsaw puzzles and cry. It broke Natalie's heart.

But having Bobo helped ease the pain. He'd chewed her favorite loafers and stained the Oriental carpet beside her bed, but one look into his baby brown eyes and she forgave him anything. During the cab ride home from Wall Street every afternoon she pictured his wriggling, joyful welcome and was almost glad her mother hadn't wanted him.

Almost. She needed to solve this problem with Alice, who refused to see either a doctor or a counselor. Gazing over the tops of the leafless trees, Natalie picked out her own lit apartment windows and her mother's two stories above that. There had to be a way to coax her mother out of this depression, if she could just think of what—

"Bobo!" She made a grab for the leash, but the puppy's unexpected leap for freedom yanked it right out of her hand. "Bobo, no!"

Leash trailing, he bounded toward the lake, intent on playing with a pair of mallards pecking a hole in the ice.

"Bobo, come back!" She ran after him, but he was already skidding across the slick surface in pursuit of the ducks. Then, with a sickening crack, he fell through.

"Bobo!" She started after him just as his head bobbed to the surface. He'd never be able to climb out again. The ice was too thin.

A strong hand gripped her arm, pulling her back. "I'll get him."

She looked into the warm brown eyes of a stranger. "But—"

"I'm a firefighter. Rescues are my job."

She glanced down at the letters on his sweatshirt— FDNY.

"Don't worry," he murmured. With a reassuring squeeze he released her arm and started out on the ice.

"He's…he's just a puppy!" she called after him.

"I know. He'll be fine."

Natalie clenched her hands under her chin. "It's okay, Bobo! The nice man's coming to get you! Keep swimming, baby!" Heart pounding, she watched the puppy struggling to keep his head above the icy water. Oh, God. He was so little.

"I'm coming, Bobo. Hang on, buddy." The firefighter inched forward, testing the ice with every step. Finally he got to his hands and knees and crawled.

Natalie winced as she imagined how cold that would be on his bare hands and through the knees of his cotton jogging pants. He must have been out for a late-afternoon run when he saw Bobo fall in. She held her breath as he eased to his stomach and stretched out his arms to the puppy. Just a little more…a little…

Crunch. A portion of ice gave way beneath his shoulders as he made a grab for the dog. When his head and shoulders went underwater, Natalie started out on the ice.

"Wait, lady!" someone yelled. "He's got him!"

She paused, just as powerful spotlights illuminated the area. In the same instant the firefighter came up with Bobo and rolled sideways to a solid patch of ice. Several people cheered, and Natalie looked around in amazement at the crowd that had gathered, including the TV crew. A camera was trained on the drenched man crawling back to the shore, a wiggling Bobo clutched under his arm.

Natalie wanted to hug the breath out of that fireman. As the terror receded she noticed he was darned cute, too. His job required him to be in shape, but she doubted the fire department required a square jaw and beautiful eyes.

When he reached a firmer patch of ice he staggered to his feet and blinked in the glare. Bobo squirmed in his arms, and he glanced down at the puppy. "I'm afraid we have an audience, sport." Snuggling Bobo against his chest he walked carefully toward where Natalie stood with her arms outstretched, wiggling her fingers impatiently.

Gratitude put a lump in her throat. "How can I ever thank you?"

He gave her a crooked grin as he handed over Bobo. "You can call off the TV guys. What's going on?"

She tucked the shivering puppy under her coat and gazed up at him. "I think they just happened to be in the area. Listen, I at least owe you dinner, or—"

His glance flicked past her. "There's a reporter headed over here with a mike. I'm gonna disappear."

"But—"

He backed away and pushed his wet hair off his forehead. "Call FDNY and ask for Jonah Hayes."

"Sir!" The reporter hurried toward them.

Jonah turned and sprinted across the frozen ground.

1

JONAH WISHED the building would catch fire.

He'd never had such a horrible thought before, but it was all that would save him from walking out on the Grand Ballroom stage at the Waldorf in front of a thousand screaming women. He was to be auctioned off tonight.

Maybe a firefighter *was* a public servant, but this was more public than he'd ever intended to get. He'd rather be headed into a bad factory fire complete with hazardous waste. But the chief had said he could do this or turn in his badge. The reputation of FDNY was at stake, according to the department's PR people, and the chief's job was on the line if he didn't make Jonah cooperate.

And all because a woman with tousled blond hair and big gray eyes had lost her grip on her puppy. Maybe if he hadn't been wearing his FDNY sweatshirt he could have stayed anonymous, but WOR had hotfooted a clip over to the main office and he'd been identified in time for the evening news. After that, life as he'd known it had ceased to exist.

On stage the bidding ended for the poor bastard ahead of him, and Jonah's throat went dry. Earlier in the evening he'd distracted himself by joking around with some of the other bachelors backstage, but as his turn grew nearer, he'd sought a spot alone to try to calm his nerves.

He reminded himself that the money was going to literacy. He'd fought a fire caused by someone who couldn't read the directions that came with a toaster oven, so he knew literacy was an important cause. He'd begged the chief to let him donate a portion of his pay for the next million years instead of getting auctioned off tonight. The chief had said he wouldn't make enough in a million years to equal the price he'd probably bring at this event. He was a local hero.

"And another six thousand dollars goes to literacy as our twenty-sixth bachelor walks out to meet the lucky lady who outbid the competition," announced the female emcee.

Six thousand, Jonah thought. That was a pile of money. He wondered what sort of woman would pay that much for a fantasy date with a stranger. Even though it was for a good cause, she'd have to be very rich and a little bit nuts. Not his type.

"We have lots more of these highly eligible men to go, so dig deep, gals. Heart Books believes every man, woman and child should have the opportunity to read, and every woman in this room should have the opportunity to date a hunk. I promise you, that's a mild description of the man who's next on the auction block."

Jonah winced. He'd never read a romance novel, but he'd never had anything against them. Until now. Murphy's Law had been working overtime for the company to be planning its bachelor auction to celebrate fifty years of publishing at the exact moment when an editor had seen him on TV fishing a lady's puppy out of the drink.

A cheer rose from the crowd, and he knew they must

have flashed a still of that puppy scene on the giant screens positioned on either side of the stage.

"Although he needs no further introduction, let me add that this valiant and tenderhearted gentleman is twenty-nine years old, graduated from SUNY with a degree in sociology, stands six-two and weighs in at a hundred and eighty-three pounds dripping wet. His hobbies include basketball and sailing, and I'm told he plays a mean game of chess."

Jonah grimaced at the *sailing* part. One of his buddies had a dinky little boat they took out once in a while, but Jonah didn't consider himself much of a sailor. The chief had insisted he put it down on the questionnaire because it sounded sexy.

The emcee continued the buildup, tightening the noose. *"As your program states, bachelor number twenty-seven comes with an afternoon sail on the Hudson followed by a breathtaking helicopter ride over the city at night. The couple will then be limoed to the Plaza, where dinner and two complimentary rooms will be provided, plus a gourmet breakfast. Let's welcome the man who's lit a fire under the entire female population of New York City, the man voted most wanted to carry us from a burning building, FDNY firefighter Jonah Hayes!"*

The blood roared in Jonah's ears as he forced himself to walk out on the stage. With luck he wouldn't pass out, although unconsciousness might be a blessing. Fortunately the spotlights blinded him to the audience seated at linen-draped tables, but he couldn't shut out the sound of their applause, the cheers or the whistling. It was a nightmare, and it was all the fault of that innocent-looking blonde he'd seen on so many afternoons in the park, walking her little black puppy.

Why couldn't she have held on to the damn leash? Then he could have stopped during his jog some afternoon and spoken to her, as he'd planned to do. If she'd been friendly, they might have had a nice normal date. Meanwhile he'd still be living his own quiet life. He'd have been able to keep his old phone number and he wouldn't be shopping for groceries at three in the morning to avoid being mobbed by women.

"And what's the first bid for this modern-day Sir Galahad?" trilled the emcee into the microphone.

"Ten thousand!" called a woman from the balcony.

Jonah almost choked. The last guy had gone for six, and they were *starting* the bid for him at ten. Good God. Who did these women think he was?

"Twelve!" shouted someone from the main floor.

"Fifteen!"

"Seventeen!"

Jonah stood in total shock as the bidding grew frenzied, rising above the cost of a medium-priced car. What could an ordinary guy like him possibly do or say in a twenty-four-hour period that would make a woman feel satisfied with that kind of investment? He was doomed.

"Thirty thousand!"

Jonah closed his eyes. Unbelievable.

"Thirty-two!"

"I have thirty-two," said the emcee, winking at him. *"Do I hear thirty-three? Come on, ladies. People say the heroes in romance novels are too good to be true. Here's living proof they're not. Who'll be the lucky woman to win New York's favorite fireman?"*

"Thirty-three!" came a bid from the back.

Jonah prayed that would be the end, and amazingly, it was. The emcee tried to coax more from the crowd, but apparently thirty-three thousand dollars was the limit. Some limit. He'd be spending a weekend with a very wealthy idiot.

An aide posted at the back of the room hurried forward with the winner's name and handed it to the emcee.

The emcee read the information on the piece of paper and glanced up with a grin. *"This is a moment right out of a romance novel, ladies, what people in the trade call a cute meet. Our lucky bidder is none other than the woman whose puppy Jonah saved from the freezing lake, Natalie LeBlanc!"*

Oh, sure she was, Jonah thought. Women had been calling the station for weeks claiming to be Natalie LeBlanc. One had even said she was Natalie's mother. He hadn't dared return any of the calls. Then women had shown up at the station with their hair dyed blond and cut short, the way Natalie's had looked on the TV clip. This was probably just another goofball looking for publicity.

The emcee motioned Jonah over to the mike and he went with great reluctance. She spoke into the mike. *"Have you and Natalie communicated since that afternoon, Jonah?"* She held it out to him.

He cleared his throat. *"No. My life since then has been a little crazy."*

"Understandably so," the emcee said. *"I'm afraid that's what you get for being such a great guy. You have our sincere gratitude, Jonah. If you'll just follow Denise, she'll escort you to Natalie. Let's have a round of applause for firefighter Jonah Hayes. We're all carrying a torch for you, gorgeous."*

Certain he was about to be the victim of some fatal attraction, Jonah allowed himself to be led off the stage and into the audience. Getting to the back of the room was no easy trick as guests left their tables to block his way. And of course, the damn TV camera preceded him, poking in his face whenever possible.

Denise was polite but firm as she eased him through the crowd. Jonah had never inhaled so much perfume in his life. Individually he might have liked many of these women. As a mob they were scary. They all wanted something—an autograph, a button off his coat, a kiss, a date, a date for their daughter. Soon the pockets of his tux coat bulged with slips of paper women had stuffed in as he went by.

As he glanced toward the back of the room, he noticed a blonde who'd done a better job than most at imitating the woman who'd lost her puppy. He looked closer. She was all decked out in a sparkly silver off-the-shoulder dress, but her hair was the way he remembered it, very light blond with a raggedy cut framing her face, making her look like a sexy urchin. As he continued toward the back of the room and got a better look, he was impressed with how much she looked like the real Natalie. It was probably the lousy lighting in the room.

She was definitely the highest bidder, because there was an empty chair pushed in next to hers at the table. His chair. But of course she wasn't really Natalie. The real Natalie wouldn't be here—not the woman who looked so cute playing with her dog, who had such expressive gray eyes, who had such an adorable turned-up nose. That person wouldn't have been stupid enough to pay thirty-three thousand dollars to be with him. She wouldn't bid on a guy like a rancher buying a prize bull to stand at stud. She wouldn't—

"Jonah," Denise said, "although you've met before,

allow me to formally introduce you to the lady who submitted the winning bid, Natalie LeBlanc."

She would.

NATALIE TRIED not to hyperventilate. She'd just cleaned out her retirement account, her nest egg, her hedge against turning into a bag lady, in the space of ten minutes. And her reward was approaching her table, much to the excitement of the women sitting with her.

"I can't believe you did this," her friend Barb said under her breath.

Natalie glanced briefly at her redheaded office partner. "I had to," she muttered. Then she turned back to Jonah, her smile firmly in place. The money didn't matter, she told herself while she tried to keep her teeth from chattering as adrenaline poured through her system.

What mattered was that her mother had seen the news clip of Jonah rescuing Bobo and had begun writing a romance novel with a firefighter as the hero. This particular firefighter, in fact. Her mother hadn't been able to reach him to ask all her research questions, and heaven knows Natalie had tried. But when she had suggested contacting other firemen, Alice seemed to think only Jonah would do.

Natalie believed this novel-writing project would do the trick. Her mother had always fantasized about being an author, but marriage to a *New York Times* book critic had sapped her courage to try. Years ago Natalie had found the first chapter of a romance her mother had started to write then abandoned for fear her intellectual husband would make fun of her. Now Alice was free to follow her dream.

By the time Natalie heard about the bachelor auction

and saw Jonah's name on the list, she was desperate. But she had to tread carefully. Her mother's budding idea was in a very tender stage, and if Jonah wasn't the sort of man to treat it with respect, then Natalie had just wasted thirty-three thousand dollars. But she mustn't think about that, or she'd run screaming from the ballroom. She'd take their weekend together to become acquainted with Jonah and find out if he was indeed the man her mother needed to bring this project to completion and end her long period of depression.

As Jonah was introduced to Natalie, he looked as if he'd seen a ghost, and not a very appealing one, either. That warmth she remembered in his brown eyes was gone. Well, he'd just been through a bit of an ordeal. A Lone Ranger type who'd run away after performing his heroic deed probably wasn't crazy about standing on a stage and being auctioned off like hamburger on the hoof.

She'd do her best to put him at ease, which would take her mind off the enormous amount of money she'd just pledged to this charity event. In the past she'd been conservative with her own investments, but that strategy might have to change if she wanted to recoup some of what she'd spent tonight.

She smiled brightly at him. "It's good to see you again, Jonah."

"Are you crazy?" The words tumbled out as if he couldn't stop them. "I'm not worth thirty-three grand!"

The other women at the table giggled and Natalie felt the heat climb to her cheeks. She glanced significantly toward the television camera trained on both of them. "Why don't we discuss that later? After the commotion dies down."

He followed the direction of her glance. "Good idea." He pulled out his chair and sat down.

A female reporter shoved a microphone toward them. "Would you comment on how it feels being reunited after that dramatic rescue in January?"

"I'm pleased to be able to thank Jonah in person for saving my dog," Natalie said.

"Thirty-three thousand is a heck of a lot of gratitude," the reporter said. "Do I sense a budding romance between you two?"

"Absolutely not," Jonah said. "We both believe in the cause of literacy, and this is a good way to support it. Now, I don't want to tell you how to do your job, but I heard backstage that the guy who's up next is the love child of Elvis and Marilyn."

"You know, I heard that rumor, too." Natalie kept her expression serious.

The reporter snatched up a program from the table and consulted it. "The guy's only listed as a member of the Heart Books' sales force."

Jonah shrugged. "You should hear his version of *Love Me Tender*. But it's up to you. I could be wrong."

The reporter sighed. "And you could be right. I've been in this business long enough to know truth is stranger than fiction. Thanks for your time." She signaled to her cameraman and started toward the front of the ballroom.

Jonah glanced at Natalie. "Thanks for the help."

"You're welcome." Natalie could tell he'd relaxed some, because as tightly as he was wedged in next to her, she could feel his tense muscles loosen as he leaned back in the chair. He had the most muscled body she'd been wedged against in some time, and to her surprise she liked it. She hadn't thought muscles mattered to her, but Jonah's physique was a definite turn-on.

Her mother should make sure to describe his muscles in the book, Natalie thought. In fact, she wondered if her mother had enough experience to imagine a love scene with a guy like this. Natalie's father had looked more like Woody Allen than Arnold Schwarzenegger. Natalie had been reading a few of the romances Heart Books published, and the men weren't built like Woody Allen. They were built like...Jonah.

"Is that guy really Elvis and Marilyn's kid?" asked one of the women at the table.

Jonah's expression remained serious. "You never know."

"You were just trying to get rid of the reporter, weren't you?" asked another. "I've been watching you. You don't like the spotlight, do you?"

"Not much."

"That's why you'd be so perfect for my Janice." A third woman whipped a picture out of her wallet and shoved it across the table. "Her phone number's on the back. She's a wonderful—"

"You know," Barb said, "I'll bet Natalie and Jonah need to get a few things settled. Why don't we excuse them a moment so they can do that?"

"Well, of course." The woman edged the picture closer to Jonah. "But if you'd just take that with you."

"I'll be glad to. You must be very proud of her." Jonah took the picture and put it in his pocket.

"Oh, I am."

"We'll just slip out to the lobby for a minute." Jonah extricated himself from the close quarters and helped Natalie with her chair.

"You won't be back," said the woman who'd given

him the picture. "I saw the way you skedaddled out of the park when they tried to interview you after the puppy rescue. I admire modesty in a man. Just don't lose that picture."

"I won't."

Natalie was beginning to understand what a huge problem she'd created for this guy when she lost her grip on Bobo's leash. He might not be inclined to do her or her mother any favors, and she wouldn't blame him. But she had to give it the old college try. She leaned down as she passed Barb's chair. "Thanks for being my buddy tonight."

Barb glanced up at her. "Got cab fare, toots?"

Natalie grinned. "Yeah, but I might have to start taking the bus. See you tomorrow at the office."

Once out of the ballroom, Jonah made a beeline for the coat check. "We can talk this out in a cab, and if you want to come back, I'll have the cab drop you. But I'm outta here."

"I understand." She hurried to keep up with his long strides.

"Oh, I doubt it, Natalie."

Maybe she didn't, Natalie thought as even the coat-check attendant fussed over Jonah. Finally they made it to the street and into a cab.

Jonah turned to her. "Where to?"

"Your place is fine."

"Whoa. My place is *not* fine. You get me for the weekend of your choice, but between now and then we won't be seeing each other socially."

She bristled. "That isn't what I meant. I only meant we can take the cab to your place, talk on the way, and then I'll take the same cab to my place after I drop you off."

"And what if I don't want you to know where I live?"

"Oh, for heaven's sake! What do you think I'm going to do, stalk you?"

He turned to face her. "I haven't the foggiest idea what you're going to do. I can't even comprehend a woman plunking down thirty-three thousand dollars to spend the weekend with Mel Gibson, let alone yours truly. Therefore I have to figure that you're a few bricks short of a load. No telling what's up with you."

"I wasn't the only one! Someone bid thirty-two thousand, and before that someone bid thirty-one, and before that…well, that was me at thirty thousand, but what about the others? Are they all crazy, too?"

"Totally. And it seems to be going around. I saved a *puppy*, for God's sake! You'd think I'd just deflected a comet that would have wiped out all of civilization. It's insane the way women have reacted."

She gazed at him in astonishment. He truly didn't know how appealing he'd looked staggering out of the lake with Bobo in his arms. He didn't understand that a single act had branded him as selfless, brave, sensitive and strong, besides being easy on the eyes. Maybe he didn't realize how women everywhere longed for that combination in a man and went a little berserk when they found it.

From his perspective, she was a weirdo with far too much money for her own good. If she put herself in his place, she might have had the same thoughts. If a guy had this much attention lavished on him and hadn't started believing his own press, he had to be something special. He might be exactly what she needed for her mother. But first she had to get him to trust her.

"Okay," she said. "I was only trying to save you cab

fare by paying for the entire ride myself. If you would rather, we can go to my place first and then you can take the cab to wherever you live. I'll pay for my leg, but you'll have to pay for yours."

"You've already paid thousands of dollars to be with me. You don't have to pick up my cab fare." He gave her a wry grin. "At least let a guy hang on to his pride."

Oh, you've hung on to more than your pride, Jonah, she thought. But she didn't speak the compliment aloud. Thinking that she was a predatory female, he would only misinterpret it. Instead she gave the driver her address and the cab pulled into traffic.

2

JONAH THOUGHT the guys at the station would get a laugh out of this one. A beautiful, rich woman had just paid thirty-three thousand dollars for the pleasure of his company and had even hinted that she'd be willing to go up to his apartment tonight. And he, being such a genius, had rejected her subtle suggestion.

The guys already thought he was nuts for turning aside all the offers that had come his way since the puppy episode, but they might look at things differently if they were walking in his size twelves. Having one or two women flirt with you was one thing. Being mobbed was something else completely.

In the past few weeks he'd become gun-shy. He expected every woman he met to make a move on him. Yet Natalie sat on her side of the cab and there was nothing predatory in her expression at all. She looked just the way he remembered her from the park, except fancier with her white fur coat, which made her look like a princess in a winter carnival.

He supposed the coat was real fur and the sparkling gems in the necklace around her slender throat were real diamonds. He'd never dated anyone who lived on Central Park West. For some reason, he hadn't thought she lived there, even if it was perfectly logical that she would since he saw her walking her dog in Central Park every afternoon. He'd wanted to believe she came from another part of town just as he did, because the area was so beautiful.

Her scent tantalized him, and for a moment he imagined what this cab ride would be like if they'd become friends in the park and decided to go out together. He'd be sitting a hell of a lot closer than he was now, that's for sure. Despite everything, he still got a charge looking into those wide gray eyes of hers. Her mouth intrigued him, too. He liked the fact that she used a pale lipstick that barely looked as if she had on any at all.

Considering all the money she'd paid, she probably wouldn't object if he slid over and tasted those pale pink lips. The idea appealed to him more than a little. But he didn't really want to go down that road, not anymore. Any woman desperate enough to spend thirty-three thousand dollars for a date had something very wrong with her. He might not see it at first, because he'd be blinded by sex, but then one night an ice pick would appear in her hand, just like with Sharon Stone in *Basic Instinct*. And Sharon was also a beautiful blonde, he reminded himself.

"Are you free this coming weekend?" she asked.

He jumped. "This weekend?"

"We have to pick a time to use the package, and unless you have a problem with this weekend, we may as well do it then."

Damn, she was eager. She might look poised and serene sitting over there in her icy white fur, but she wasn't wasting any time getting with the program. But he'd have chaperons around the whole time, so he should be relatively safe. Someone else was going to sail the expensive yacht down the Hudson, thank God, and someone else would fly the helicopter. After that they'd be at the Plaza with lots of other people. He just had to be sure she didn't somehow get his room key.

"I guess this coming weekend would be okay." Actually, the chief's words had been *"Take whatever time off you need."* It was a bone he was throwing Jonah's way in exchange for making his existence a living hell.

"You think I'm absolutely insane, don't you?" she asked.

He wondered if telling a crazy person that they were crazy was a bad idea. "It's crossed my mind."

"I don't blame you." She smiled. "I would think the same thing in your position."

He was fascinated by her mouth. What a terrific smile she had. What a kissable mouth. He'd never made love to someone who'd gone around the bend. Maybe it would be fantastic...until they killed you or cut off something important.

"You probably won't believe this," she continued, "but I'm a perfectly normal woman. I've been wanting to tell you how grateful I am that you saved Bobo, but I couldn't reach you. When I read about this auction, it seemed like the perfect gesture."

"You could have sent flowers to the station, like six hundred or so other women did."

She started to laugh. "You got *six hundred* bouquets?"

"About. Maybe more like six-fifty. After all the guys took them home to their wives, mothers and sweethearts, we still had some left, so we made deliveries to the nursing homes. Except I couldn't go."

"Why not?"

"I did the first time, but the sweet little ladies wouldn't let me leave, and they started to cry when I finally made my way toward the door. It was too horrible. I couldn't put myself through it again."

She shook her head, her eyes filled with sympathy. "Bobo and I really caused a big problem for you, didn't we?"

"You have no idea. But the whole thing was beginning to die down. People don't stay interested forever. Then along comes this bachelor auction. Now I'm afraid it will all start up again."

"What can I do to help?"

He almost believed she wanted to help him. Without realizing it he'd moved closer to her, drawn by her laughter and apparent understanding. "Just tell me what you want," he said, gazing into her eyes.

"To get to know you," she murmured in a husky voice.

When she talked in that intimate tone of voice, he couldn't help watching her mouth and wondering what it would be like to touch those pink lips. "You paid all that money just to get to know me?"

"I had no choice. You were unreachable."

"I know." But she was very reachable right now, and touching her coat was like stroking a kitten. "Lots of women pretended to be you."

"They did?"

He slid his hand back and forth along the collar of her coat. "They tried to copy your special look."

Her mouth tipped up to his and her lips parted ever so slightly. "I don't have a special look."

"Yes, you do."

"I'm just an ordinary girl."

"I don't think so." He couldn't stand it. He had to brush his mouth against hers, just once. Her lips were like velvet. He came back a second time to make sure they were really that soft. They were even softer, coaxing him to stay. He cradled the back of her head and got serious. Perfect.

Fleetingly he thought that this was probably how Sharon Stone got Michael Douglas to cooperate. Then he stopped thinking as she opened to him and his body tightened a little more with each slow exploration of his tongue. He slid his hand down the nape of her neck beneath her coat collar and stroked her warm skin. Images of running his hands all over her body played in his mind until he was short of breath and straining the fly of his tux pants.

The cabdriver cleared his throat.

Jonah released Natalie with a start. The taxi was no longer running, not that he would have noticed. He'd forgotten they were in a cab. He'd forgotten that this was the woman who had bid an enormous amount of money to chain herself to his side for the weekend. He'd forgotten she probably carried an ice pick in her garter.

Her gaze was unfocused and dreamy. "That was… very nice."

"At the going rate, that was probably about a five-hundred-dollar kiss."

Her dreaminess evaporated and she frowned. "Could you do me a favor and forget about the money?"

"Not likely."

"Well, I'd appreciate it if you'd try." She opened the cab door and glanced over at him. "Want to come up and see Bobo? He's grown quite a bit since that afternoon at the park."

Lust warred with reason as he gazed longingly at her tempting mouth. "Better not."

"Suit yourself. See you this weekend." She handed the driver some money and got out of the cab. Then she leaned down and peeked in at Jonah. "Sure you won't change your mind? I make a mean cup of cappuccino."

He wanted in the worst way to go with her, because he thought they stood a good chance of making more than cappuccino if he did. But then who knew what would happen after that? Despite what she said, she was no ordinary girl. And apartments had kitchens, and kitchens had knives. "Thanks, but I have to report in early tomorrow morning," he said.

"Okay." With a last dazzling smile, she closed the door and walked up to the apartment entrance where a uniformed doorman tipped his hat and opened the door for her.

"Where to?" the cabbie asked.

Jonah gave him his considerably less impressive address. The cabbie blew out a breath and shook his head, obviously mystified by Jonah's stupidity. Reflecting on that kiss as the cab pulled away, Jonah felt pretty stupid, himself. Maybe some things were worth taking a chance for.

NATALIE HAD JUST TAKEN Bobo for his early-morning walk and was putting water in the coffeepot when someone pounded on her door. The dog raced into the foyer, barking with excitement. Natalie hurried after him and looked through the peephole into the hall to make sure it was her mother standing on the other side of the door.

Sure enough, an elongated version of Alice LeBlanc was tapping a copy of the *New York Times* against her palm. She must have charged down in the elevator immediately after reading about Natalie's bid because she still wore her pink chenille bathrobe, and her gray-streaked hair looked as if it had been styled with an electric mixer. Her reading glasses were perched on the end of her nose.

Natalie unlocked the door and opened it. "Well, good—"

"What on earth have you done? Are you crazy? Hello, Bobo." Her mother marched past both daughter and dog and whirled to face them. "Thirty-three thousand dollars? What did you do, clean out your IRA?"

"Yep." Natalie made a production out of relocking the door to get her racing heart under control before she met her mother's gaze. Every time she thought of her empty retirement fund she pictured an old age spent at the Salvation Army.

"Are you insane?" Her mother peered over the top of her glasses. "Please tell me this doesn't have anything to do with me."

"It doesn't have anything to do with you," Natalie lied, knowing the truth would fill her mother with guilt. "I've been fantasizing about that guy, just like every other woman in New York, and I couldn't get through to him, either."

"Yes, but isn't this a bit extreme?"

"Extreme situations call for extreme measures. I have more reason to be smitten than the women who only saw him on TV. I interacted with him up close and personal, and I…fell a little bit in love during that episode at the lake, if you must know. I realize love at first sight is considered naive, but when I turned and looked into his eyes for the first time, it was… amazing." Not amazing enough to spend her retirement money on, but he definitely had a way about him. That mesmerizing gaze of his had made her forget herself for a moment in the cab last night.

"Oh, sweetheart." Her mother tossed aside the paper and came over to enfold Natalie in her arms while Bobo scampered around them in delight. "Of course I believe in love at first sight, but it usually doesn't cost thirty-three thousand dollars. What must Jonah think of a woman who would do something like this?"

Natalie hugged her back, grateful that this auction business seemed to be distracting her mother from her grief. That alone was worth the money. "Jonah thinks I'm crazy," Natalie said.

Her mother held her firmly by the shoulders, exactly the way she'd done when Natalie was eight years old and in big trouble. "That's not a very good beginning."

"I know." As she considered beginnings, Natalie thought about the kiss last night in the cab. Nice as it had been, it probably wasn't a very good beginning, either. She'd bid on Jonah to get his cooperation to help her mother. Kissing him was liable to distract her from her goal.

"Does he realize you sacrificed your old-age fund to get a date with him?"

Natalie wished her mother would stop bringing up a subject that made her queasy. She responded with a confident smile. "I'm a stockbroker, Mom. With a few well-chosen investments, I can start making the money back in no time. I'll just use a more aggressive approach for a while." If only she felt as sure of that as she sounded. She headed for the kitchen. "I need to feed Bobo. Want some coffee?"

Alice followed her. "So if Jonah doesn't know you threw away your retirement account—"

"I didn't throw it away." Natalie poured dog food

into Bobo's bowl and scooped some coffee beans into the hand grinder. "Heart Books staged the auction to benefit literacy, and that's a very good cause."

Alice waited for the noise of the grinding to stop. "You don't have to tell me that, after being married to a literary critic for thirty years."

"I guess not." Natalie held her breath, wondering if the reference to her late husband would send Alice into a bout of weeping. It had happened plenty of times before.

"Still, I doubt Heart Books or the literacy movement expected anyone to surrender their nest egg in the name of a good cause," her mother finished calmly.

Natalie relaxed. Apparently this fascinating new subject of the bachelor auction had claimed her mother's full attention. "I'd hoped the bidding for Jonah wouldn't go that high, but Mom, you should have seen those women. They went bonkers for him."

Alice perched on a stool at the breakfast bar. "And so you went super-bonkers. Does he think you have this kind of money to throw around?"

"Probably." She started the coffee brewing. "He also knows I live here, and I didn't bother to explain about Great-Uncle Jerome and all that rent-control stuff."

"Oh, boy. So he thinks the way everyone else does— that we're rolling in it."

"Actually he thinks I'm rolling in it. He doesn't know you live in this building. And I'd rather have him think I'm rich than to have him know I spent my savings on him. Then he'd really question my sanity. Toast?"

Alice nodded. "Thanks." She tapped her finger against her mouth and frowned. "So," she said at last, "you need to get him to fall in love with you, even though he thinks you're some spoiled rich woman who buys a boy toy when she gets bored."

"I guess that's about the size of it." Or at least the version she wanted her mother to believe.

Her mother smiled. "That should be easy. Just be yourself. You're not a spoiled rich girl, and that will become obvious the longer he's with you. And once he's truly in love with you, you can tell him the truth."

"The truth?" Natalie was losing sight of what that was, exactly.

"That you have no retirement fund and are, in fact, a financial liability. That should arouse his protective instincts considering he put you in this sorry mess because he's such an Adonis. So that should be that. Happily ever after."

"That was more or less my plan." Except that Jonah didn't have to fall madly in love with her. He only had to like her enough to go along with her mother's project.

"You know, this would make a neat plot twist in my novel," her mother said. "A bachelor auction. I hadn't even thought of it, but I could probably work it in."

Natalie concentrated on buttering the toast so her mother wouldn't notice her smile of triumph. "Maybe so."

"And if you win him over, which I have no doubt you can do because your motives are pure, I might even be able to interview him and clear up a few details in my book."

Natalie kept buttering. She wasn't so sure about pure motives, but she believed they were noble ones, at any rate. "We'll see, Mom. I can't promise anything, but we'll see."

"I'm still shocked about the money, though. You've

been contributing to your retirement account since you graduated from college, and I was always impressed with your foresight."

Natalie looked at her, glad she could finally say something honest for a change. "What's more important, financial security or connecting with those you love?"

"You know my answer. But it's a good thing your father isn't around to hear about this. He'd hit the ceiling. I'm sure he would never have understood such youthful impetuosity."

"But you do?"

Her mother studied her with fondness in her blue eyes. "Of course I do. Why do you suppose I've decided to write a romance?"

A TOTAL OF FOUR GUYS from the station contributed to Jonah's wardrobe for the weekend. The sailing date wouldn't be a problem, clotheswise, but Jonah wasn't accustomed to being limoed to the Plaza and treated as an honored guest there. Stewart came up with a dinner jacket, Herm produced a silk tie, Billy happened to have a good leather belt in Jonah's size and Cal loaned Jonah his topcoat, the same one Jonah had worn over the rented tux for the bachelor auction.

There was much debate among the firefighters as to whether Jonah should buy new underwear for the occasion. No matter how many times Jonah declared that he wasn't going to engage in any activities in which underwear would be a factor, the men still insisted he should be prepared. Red was the favored color, and there were also some helpful suggestions about birth control and bedroom technique.

Jonah hadn't felt so fussed over since his senior

prom, and he remembered not liking that much, either. Even his parents had called from Buffalo to see if he needed anything for his big date. He almost told them that a well-trained bodyguard would be a good idea.

It amazed him that everyone seemed to think it was perfectly understandable that a lady had spent thirty-three thousand for a date with him. His mother said that amount was about what a date with him was worth, because he was a real prize. Apparently she never considered that the lady in question might be totally wacko.

As Jonah packed his small suitcase on Saturday morning, he deliberately left out the red underwear Herm had presented him with. The glow-in-the-dark condoms definitely weren't going. As long as he didn't pack birth control, he wouldn't be tempted to get carried away, and after that kiss he'd shared with Natalie, he knew that getting carried away was a possibility.

On the cab ride to the pier, he thought some more about that kiss. To be honest with himself, he'd thought about being with Natalie more than he should have. He'd been eager for Saturday to arrive so that he could see her again. Not that he would kiss her again. You didn't kiss a woman like Natalie when you were going to spend the weekend with her unless you were willing to go where that kiss would inevitably lead.

He became aroused just thinking of where it could lead. Okay, so he was willing. More than willing. But he didn't believe in making love to a woman for a temporary thrill, he told himself sternly. That's all it could be with someone like Natalie, whose life and priorities were so different from his. And he had to keep in mind that she was nuts.

That would be difficult, he thought as he climbed

from the cab and saw her leaning against the railing of the sleek yacht. She lifted her face to the warmth of the sun, and it shone on her wind-tossed blond hair. Someone had ordered up a perfect spring day for this sail and Natalie had responded by wearing all white. Her slacks, blouse and the sweatshirt she'd knotted by the sleeves around her shoulders gave her an almost virginal look. She seemed to glow as she stood on the polished wooden deck.

He remembered how irresistible she'd been when he was with her in the cab and that kissing her had seemed like the only option. Damned if he didn't want to kiss her again, and the day was just beginning.

"Sir?"

"Hmm?" Jonah snapped out of his daze and glanced at a guy in khakis and a shirt with *Satin Doll* embroidered on the breast pocket.

"My name is Eric. Welcome aboard the *Satin Doll*. Would you like me to take your luggage?"

"Sure. Thanks." Jonah handed him the small suitcase and crossed the gangplank.

Natalie turned to him and waved. "Isn't this glorious?"

"Beautiful day." He swallowed. Even her voice tempted him. He had no idea how he'd manage to keep his hands off her for the next twenty-four hours. Taking a deep breath and adjusting his sunglasses, he walked toward the bow of the boat.

Just as he reached Natalie, a woman also wearing the yacht's name on her shirt approached them. "Welcome to the *Satin Doll*. My name's Suzanne. What can I get each of you to drink?"

"Champagne!" announced Natalie with a big grin.

Jonah shrugged. Her enthusiasm was contagious. "Why not?"

"I'll be right back," Suzanne said, and left.

Natalie looked like a kid at a carnival. "This is so exciting. Do you suppose they'll let us take the wheel?"

He leaned his forearms against the mahogany railing. He did his best to appear relaxed, although his heart was hammering from being this close to her. "I don't know. This is a pretty fancy boat."

"Yeah, but your hobby is sailing. You could convince them to let you, don't you think?"

He turned more fully toward her. Time for her to start realizing he wasn't the superhero she thought he was. That might keep both of them from making fools of themselves this weekend. "My chief made me put that down on the form, but I really don't know much about sailing. A guy from the station has a little boat and he's taken me out a few times, but I'm not qualified to sail a beauty like this."

She gazed up at him, her smile serene, her eyes hidden behind sunglasses. "If they gave an award for the most modest man in America, I'll bet you'd win, hands down."

"I'm not modest, I'm truthful. I hope you haven't bought into all the hype about me, because if you did, you're going to be sadly disappointed in the next twenty-four hours."

Her smile wavered just the tiniest bit. "I hope not," she murmured.

He almost groaned aloud. She did have high expectations for this date, after all. She probably expected some combination of Brad Pitt and Tom Cruise. He was in big trouble.

"There they are! On the *Satin Doll!*"

With a fresh feeling of dread, Jonah turned toward the dock, and sure enough, a television van had pulled up and a camera crew was piling out.

"Let's go below," he said, grabbing Natalie's arm.

"At least until we get out on the river," she agreed as the yacht moved away from the mooring slip. She started down the steps into the cabin.

"I don't think leaving the dock's going to help." Jonah glanced back at the camera crew as they boarded a motor launch. "Dammit, I was hoping this wouldn't happen. Why can't they leave me alone?"

Natalie looked over her shoulder at him. "You really don't get it, do you?"

"No! I'm nothing special."

When they reached the bottom of the steps, she took off her sunglasses and gazed at him. "I think you're wrong."

"Ah, there you are." Suzanne emerged from the galley and handed them each a champagne flute. Then she returned with the rest of the bottle nestled into an ice bucket and a tray of chocolate-covered strawberries. "Let me know if I can get you anything else." She set the bucket and tray on a table anchored in front of a leather banquette. "Lunch will be served on deck in a half hour. Listen for the bell. And enjoy!" She climbed the steps to the deck, leaving them alone.

Natalie raised her glass and touched the rim to his. "To friendship."

Jonah looked into her eyes and wondered if her motivations were that simple. Somehow he doubted it.

3

SHE REALLY DID NEED a friend, Natalie thought as she looked into Jonah's eyes. A friend who would help her mother reenter the world of the living. And she specifically needed Jonah to be that friend.

But just as it had been that night in the cab, friendship was being nudged aside by something a little more exciting. She really couldn't let that happen, at least not until she'd talked to him about her mother's book.

Jonah handed her his drink. "If you'll hold this a minute, I'll go topside and see if the TV motor launch is still after us."

"Sure." Their fingers touched as she took his glass. Yep, the chemistry was strong between them. Watching him bound up the steps to the deck made her go all warm and tight inside. She would just have to ignore the feeling and concentrate on becoming Jonah's good buddy instead. Maybe they could play chess.

Putting both champagne flutes on the table, she poked around the cabin but didn't turn up a chessboard. Finally she gave up. Untying the sleeves of her sweatshirt, she hung it on an ornate hook by the door before sliding onto the leather banquette and nestling among the pillows tossed there.

The gentle rocking motion of the boat coaxed her to lean back, put her feet up and relax. After all, she should try to enjoy herself a little, considering she'd sacrificed her retirement account to be here. She'd ordered the champagne in hopes it would make her forget about the money. And here she was not even drinking it.

She picked up her drink and helped herself to a chocolate-covered strawberry. This wasn't half-bad, she thought, biting through the chocolate into sweet red pulp. If she could forget how much this weekend was costing her, maybe she'd enjoy being pampered for a change.

As a young and inexperienced woman in the stock market, she'd had to hustle the past few years to keep her head above water. Even with her rent held lower than the other tenants' because of an old agreement made by her great-uncle, she still didn't have lots of cash for luxuries left over at the end of each month. Lately she'd been spending all her spare money and energy trying to lift her mother's depression.

At least that was working. Whenever Alice wasn't wrestling the bachelor-auction theme into her manuscript, she was brainstorming ways for Natalie to make a good impression on Jonah this weekend. The white outfit had been Alice's idea. The illusion of purity always fascinated a man, she'd said.

Meanwhile, Natalie struggled to keep her two roles straight. In her mother's presence she had to pretend to be crazy in love with Jonah, but in Jonah's presence she had to squelch any sexual feelings, or risk compromising her mission. Her brain was tired from the effort, come to think of it. She ought to have another strawberry.

She closed her eyes and took a bite. When the juice spurted out, she tried to catch the runoff with her tongue before it dribbled down her chin. She missed. Damn. She should have been more careful. Her illusion of purity was probably compromised. Opening her eyes, she glanced down at the front of her blouse. A red dot marked the exact position of her left nipple. She grabbed a napkin and started dabbing at it, which only spread the stain and made her nipple pucker under the soft material.

A soft sound drew her attention to the stairs, and she realized Jonah had been standing there for several seconds. Even across the distance separating them, she could feel the heat in his gaze. Unfortunately her body was responding to that heat. This buddy plan wasn't working too well.

He cleared his throat and walked over to sit on the opposite end of the banquette. He picked up his champagne glass and drained it before he spoke. "The launch is still keeping up with us. The captain says there's not much he can do about it, as long as they don't come close enough to be any kind of navigational danger."

"So what do you think we should do?" It came out sounding much more suggestive than she'd meant it to. She couldn't help it if being nervous made her voice husky. And she was definitely a wee bit nervous being alone with him. The look he'd given her a minute ago hadn't worn off yet, either.

He put down his glass and turned, his glance dropping to the red spot on her blouse, then moving back to her face. "I think you'd better tell me what you expect for your thirty-three thousand."

"I—I don't know what you mean."

"Then I'll be more clear. Do you expect that before this weekend is over I'll make love to you?"

The idea sent a thrill of reaction through her system. "Of course not! What sort of woman do you think I am?"

"Damned if I know!" He scooted across the banquette and leaned toward her. "And if you don't want sex, I have no earthly idea what you *do* expect for your thirty-three grand, lady. It's making me nervous."

Her chin came up. "All I expect is a fun weekend."

He leaned closer, obviously ready for a fight. "And what, may I ask, is your definition of fun?"

She got right in his face, irritated with his automatic assumptions about her. "Probably the same as yours, buster." Even if she was mad at him, he smelled nice. And she'd never noticed that freckle high on his cheekbone, or the way his lashes curled.

"I doubt it." His eyes darkened. "I can just imagine what sort of wild, exotic experience you'd consider worth all that money."

"Oh, can you?" She thought maybe his imagination was affecting his breathing, because it wasn't much steadier than hers.

He drifted closer still, and his voice took on a husky tone. "We might as well settle the main issue right now."

"I'm all for that." She loved watching his mouth, and the dimple that flashed in his cheek when he talked.

"I have…absolutely…no intention…of making love to you."

"That's good, because I have absolutely…no intention…of making love to you…either."

His kiss came hard and fast, but not fast enough to suit her. She wanted to be gobbled up, consumed by the fire. He plunged his tongue deep, and she moaned with delight. This was good, very good. Pushing her down against the leather bench, he began working at the buttons of her blouse as he continued to kiss her breathless.

She pulled his knit shirt from the waistband of his slacks and ran her hands up underneath to feel the play of muscles across his broad back. To touch him was heaven. And to be touched was...unbelievable. She gasped as he unfastened her bra and cupped her breast in his supple fingers. It was the right touch, the one she'd waited for, dreamed of, thought might be an illusion.

Bells rang. Or rather, one bell rang, quite persistently.

He lifted his mouth from hers.

Slowly she opened her eyes to gaze up at him.

"Lunch," he murmured.

She struggled to speak. "Let's...skip it."

"If we..." He paused to take a deep breath. "If we don't go up, they're liable to come down after us."

"Oh."

He stroked his thumb across her nipple. "I meant what I said."

"Okay." Her eyes fluttered closed as she absorbed the ecstasy of that gentle caress. "About what?"

"I'm not going to make love to you."

She clenched her jaw. She'd gone and forgotten her mission again. This was going to be a tougher assignment than she'd thought. "That's good, because I'm not going to make love to you, either."

"You're not?" He sounded disappointed.

She opened her eyes and strengthened her resolve. "Nope."

"Is that reverse psychology?"

"It's the truth."

"So no matter how I coaxed you, you'd say no."

"That's right." Scooting out from under him, she sat up and reached behind her back to refasten her bra.

He cleared his throat. "Well, then we both understand each other."

"I think we do." She glanced down at the stain on her blouse. It should be put to soak or it might be permanent, and this was a good blouse.

"I'm glad we cleared the air and settled everything."

"Me, too." She'd just take the blouse off and rinse it, she decided.

"And I think it's—what are you doing?"

"Taking off my blouse. What does it look like?"

"Natalie, please don't do that."

"I need to put it in some water to soak or it will be ruined." Carrying the blouse, she walked back to the galley.

"How do you expect me to stick to my decision if you're going to parade around practically naked?"

"Doesn't matter. I'm sticking to mine. But if it bothers you so much, why don't you bring me my sweatshirt?"

"Okay."

She found a little liquid soap and rubbed it vigorously into the spot.

"Here's your sweatshirt."

She glanced up and noticed his gaze riveted on her cleavage.

He shoved the sweatshirt at her. "Please."

She dried her hands on a nearby towel and took the sweatshirt. "Thanks." Then she pulled it over her head and fluffed her hair with her fingers.

He leaned in the doorway of the galley, watching her. "I like your hair."

"Me, too. Just wash, dry and go."

He nodded, as if he approved of that approach. "Why are you worried about the blouse? Couldn't you just buy another one?"

"I don't operate that way. I like this blouse, and I might not find another one exactly like it, so I'd rather take care of this one and make sure I have it for a while."

He gazed at her, his expression speculative. "You don't talk like rich women usually talk. Or the way I imagine they would."

"Maybe you're stereotyping."

"Maybe I am." He pushed away from the doorjamb. "Let's go up on deck and have some lunch."

"The TV people may still be hanging around."

He shrugged those broad shoulders. "Then they'll get boring footage of two people eating."

"Maybe you're right." Besides, she had to get out of this cozy little cabin. She headed for the stairs. "Maybe the best way to get rid of them is to go up there and demonstrate there's nothing going on between us."

"Yeah, right."

Something in his tone made her glance back at him.

He looked defensive. "Okay, I think it's stupid that you paid all that money to spend time with me, but I have to admit it's kind of a turn-on, too."

"No, really?" She gave him an exaggerated look of surprise and breezed past him up the stairs.

LUNCH WAS SOMETHING right out of the movies, Jonah thought, and he was sitting across from a starlet in casual clothes and dark glasses. To complete the illusion, they had a camera crew keeping pace with the *Satin Doll*.

"Just ignore them," Natalie said. She picked up a jumbo shrimp and dipped it in cocktail sauce.

"I guess you're right." He thanked Suzanne, who'd just refilled his champagne flute. Then he spread a cracker with warm Brie. "Why should we ruin a great meal like this worrying about being on *Candid Camera?*" Natalie looked terrific, he thought. The breeze ruffled her short hair and brought a pink blush to her cheeks.

Or maybe the blush had something to do with that scene in the cabin. God, she was hot. Apparently she was as turned on by this bizarre situation as he was. Maybe that was her motivation in the first place, to buy a guy for the weekend and tease him to death. She could be into power.

If so, she was on a roll. Watching her dip another plump shrimp in cocktail sauce and nibble her way to the tail was giving him an erection.

"Do you have a job?" he asked. Mundane conversation might keep his mind off sex.

"Of course." She wiped her fingers on her napkin. "I'm a stockbroker."

"You must be pretty good at it."

"I do okay." She peeled a leaf from her steamed artichoke and dipped it in melted butter. "How about you? I know all firefighters don't do the same job. What's your specialty?"

He struggled to remember her question as she raked the meat off the artichoke leaf with her even white teeth. Either all the food was designed to be sensuous or he was becoming obsessed. "I'm the forcible-entry man."

"Really?" Her mouth turned up at the corners. "That sounds very macho."

"It's not."

"Of course you wouldn't think so, Mr. Modest." She glanced over his shoulder. "I hate to tell you this, but there's another motorboat on the other side of us, and somebody's got a video camera pointed in our direction. They're probably just tourists who think we're famous."

"Or they work for a tabloid." Jonah didn't bother to turn around. No use letting them have a good shot of his face. "Don't you think this is getting out of hand?"

"Yeah, but what can we do about it?" She reached for another jumbo shrimp. "At least they're not making much noise."

A helicopter headed their way.

"Guess again," Jonah shouted as the helicopter swooped overhead, turned and made another pass.

Natalie glanced up at the helicopter as she chewed her shrimp. "Unbelievable," she said as she swallowed and glanced back at him. Then her eyes widened and she started to gasp for air.

Jonah's chair crashed to the deck as he leaped around the table and pulled her out of her seat. Circling her in his arms, he clasped his hands under her breastbone and applied quick upward pressure. Her sunglasses flew off and the piece of shrimp that had lodged in her windpipe sailed across the table and landed on the deck.

Suzanne and Eric hurried toward them.

"Is she okay?" Eric asked.

"I think she'll be fine in a minute." Jonah supported Natalie gently as she took several long, shaky breaths.

"Wow. I've never seen anybody react that quick."

Suzanne picked up Natalie's sunglasses. "No wonder you're a hero."

"I'm definitely not a hero," Jonah said. "Anybody would have—"

"Not true," Natalie said, her voice slightly hoarse as she extricated herself and turned to him. "Not just anybody would have saved my dog, either." She cleared her throat and gave him a tremulous smile. "First my dog, now me. It seems I owe you a great deal, Jonah." A warm light shone in her eyes.

"You don't owe me a thing." But as he looked in her eyes, he wondered what form her gratitude might take, and if he'd be strong enough to refuse it.

IN THE FACE OF Jonah's heroic and sexy persona, Natalie struggled to keep sight of her original goal. She needed to get her mother's request on the table soon, before she accidentally forgot herself again and ended up in his arms. But she hadn't figured out exactly how to broach the subject. She still wasn't sure Jonah would cooperate, especially if he thought he'd be identified somehow as the hero of the novel.

To give herself time to think, she suggested they spend the rest of the afternoon on deck, and Jonah readily agreed. That helped some, until Jonah got his chance to take the wheel. Natalie watched him grin with pleasure as he guided the sleek craft up the river, and she began to ache something fierce. Keeping her distance wasn't the easiest job she'd ever had.

Except for the helicopter that continued to dog their progress and the boats cruising alongside the yacht, the day was perfect. The sky looked as if someone had scrubbed it that morning before turning on the sunlight, and the wind blew enough to fill the sails without blasting the passengers off the deck. The new green of spring covered the hillsides along the river, and Natalie had a moment's daydream of sailing the boat all the way to Lake Champlain, alone with Jonah.

But that wasn't her goal, so she had to be glad they had chaperons galore. They kept the conversation light. As they passed Sleepy Hollow they compared notes on how much the Headless Horseman had scared them as kids. That led to a discussion of childhood, and she found out he was the oldest of four and an Eagle Scout. He learned that she was an only child who had never made it past Brownies.

At one point she slipped in the information that her father had died six months earlier, and the look of sympathy in his eyes made her want to snuggle in his arms, but she didn't. Besides, the cameras still rolled, and she'd begun to resent them almost as much as Jonah did.

On the trip back, they took turns going below and changing into their dinner clothes. Jonah went first, and the whole time he was belowdecks Natalie imagined him undressing. No matter how she tried to distract herself, she pictured what he'd look like without his shirt, without his pants, without a stitch on that glorious body.

Jonah's transformation to dinner jacket and tie made her catch her breath.

"Am I okay?" he asked as he joined her on deck.

She looked him up and down. "More than okay," she said with a smile.

But when it was her turn to appear in her red cocktail dress, she was a bundle of nerves. She never remembered caring so much how a man reacted to her outfit. Twilight had arrived by the time she stepped out on deck, and Jonah stood at the railing gazing at the jeweled skyline of the city slipping by. He must have heard the click of her heels, because he turned as she started toward him.

He didn't say a word as he held out his hand. She should have ignored his gesture. Touching him was a dangerous occupation, even with chaperons around preparing the yacht for docking. When she placed her hand in his firm grip, she looked into his eyes and her heartbeat quickened. There was no mistaking the message in his eyes, no matter what he had promised her or himself. He wanted her.

"Do I look okay?" There was that husky nervousness again.

"*Okay* doesn't even come close to describing how you look," he said, drawing her over beside him as he returned his attention to the sparkle of lights. He stared at the skyline as his hand tightened over hers. "If you planned to seduce me this weekend, you're doing a hell of a job."

"Believe me, I didn't plan to do that."

He glanced down at her. "Then I guess you're just a natural."

She looked away from his compelling gaze and swallowed. As she focused on the lights of Manhattan, she prayed she'd be able to keep her wits about her for just a few hours more. Soon she'd find the right moment to tell him about her mother's book. *Soon.*

4

AN IVORY STRETCH LIMO sat at the dock, apparently waiting for them. So was another television van and a crowd of women holding signs proclaiming their love of Jonah. He winced. "Looks like we won't be sneaking over to the heliport."

Natalie pulled her white furry coat closer against the evening chill. "Nope, but once we're in that chopper, we should be okay. It'll just be the pilot and us, high above this nonsense. I have to admit it gets old fast."

Jonah glanced at her, wondering just how much she'd like to ditch this public performance. He was forming some ideas about how they might do that. "It'll be a zoo again once we hit the Plaza."

"I suppose." Natalie sighed as Eric lowered the gangplank of the *Satin Doll*. "When I was a little girl, I wanted to be a movie star. But if this is what it's like, I'm glad it turned out I couldn't act."

Suzanne approached them. "Thank you for sailing with us," she said.

"It was great," Jonah said. "Thanks for letting me take the wheel for a while. She handles like a dream."

"You're welcome." Suzanne hesitated. "Could I— would you give me your autograph, Jonah? It's for my daughter," she said quickly, pulling a piece of paper and a pen from her slacks pocket. "Her name's

Gretchen, and she just got a little black puppy. She named him Bobo, and she would be thrilled if—"

"Sure." Jonah took the pen and paper before the moment dragged on any longer. He wrote a quick note to Gretchen and handed everything back to Suzanne. "And please tell Gretchen that you met me and I'm not seven feet tall, and I don't leap tall buildings in a single bound."

Suzanne smiled. "I was planning to tell her you're a great guy, just as wonderful as she imagines you are."

A flush worked its way up from his neck. "Uh, thanks. Well, I guess we'd better get going. Ready, Natalie?"

She glanced at him, a twinkle in her gray eyes. "Are you certain you can't fly? It would sure come in handy right now to be able to go right over the heads of all those people on the dock."

"Very funny." He glanced at Eric, who had a grip on their overnight cases and seemed ready to run interference for them. "Say, Eric, where were you figuring on stashing those?" he asked.

"In the trunk of the limo," Eric said. "Would you rather have them up with you?"

"I just want to keep this operation simple," Jonah said. "So let's not bother with the trunk. Just heave them in and we'll jump in right afterward."

"Got it."

Jonah took a deep breath. "Okay, let's go." He wrapped a protective arm around Natalie's shoulders and lowered his head against the glare from the lights as they stepped off the gangplank. "We're not stopping."

"Right."

Holding her tight against him, he shouldered his

way through the crowd behind Eric, ignoring the camera lenses, microphones and shouted questions. Ahead of him the uniformed limo driver opened the passenger door. Eric put the overnight cases inside and jumped back just as Jonah shoved Natalie in.

"Get in and drive!" Jonah shouted to the chauffeur, who seemed to think he had to hold the door for Jonah, too. Jonah leaped in and wrestled the door shut as someone tried to keep him from closing it. At last the locks clicked into place and he sagged with relief as the car edged away from the crowd.

"Are you okay?" Natalie sat in the far corner, looking small and vulnerable, her eyes wide.

"I'm okay." He didn't see any obvious scrapes or bruises on her delicate skin. "Are you?"

"Physically. But it sure messes with your head, being part of a mob scene like that, doesn't it?"

Jonah closed his eyes and leaned back against the plush upholstery. "Yep." He took a deep breath. "You know what's the worst part?"

"What?"

He kept his eyes closed and willed his tense muscles to relax. "I was raised to be polite, to respond to people with courtesy when they approached me. I can't do that anymore, because now everyone wants something."

"I...guess they do."

"And then I see some of the looks on the faces of those women, and my heart goes out to them. They need someone to speak a kind word to them, to smile, to ask them how they're doing. And I don't dare."

He felt a light touch on his arm and opened his eyes. Natalie had scooted over next to him and rested her hand on the sleeve of his sport coat. "That's one of the sweetest things I've ever heard anyone say."

God, she was beautiful, especially when she got that soft look in her eyes. The leather seat reminded him of the one down in the cabin of the boat, which reminded him of what she'd felt like beneath him. He wanted her in his arms again, wanted to kiss her and touch her the way he had this morning. "I wasn't trying to be sweet. I just—"

"You just can't help it," she said. "You're a decent human being, and so you just can't help being such a nice guy."

He sat up straighter and smiled at her. "Don't push it. I wasn't having such sweet thoughts about you just now."

Her cheeks grew rosy and she glanced down at his sleeve. Slowly she removed her hand. "You know, I'm not so different from all those women you've been trying to stay away from."

"You mean aside from the fact that you're twenty times better-looking than any of them, and probably twenty times richer, and you've promised not to go to bed with me under any circumstance? Other than that, yeah, I guess you're just like them."

The blush on her cheeks deepened and she glanced away. "I am. I want something, just like they do."

Aha. He'd been afraid from the beginning that she had an agenda. He'd hoped to be wrong, but apparently not. He wondered if it was something kinky, or illegal, or kinky *and* illegal. She looked innocent enough, but he'd only spent a few hours with her. How could he claim to know whether that innocence was a cover-up for all sorts of weird cravings? And damned if the idea didn't excite him. Even straight arrows could be tempted.

As his imagination worked overtime, his question came out sounding gruffer than he'd meant it to. "What do you want?"

She glanced at him uncertainly. "Maybe this isn't the time to discuss it."

"That wild, huh?"

"No, it's just—"

"Just what?" he asked softly, his heart pounding. He should have guessed that a woman with her looks and her money had become bored with traditional sex. She probably didn't want to go to bed with him because she was saving him for something far more elaborate than a simple roll in the hay. When he'd asked if she expected him to make love to her this weekend, she'd probably laughed to herself at his conventional ideas.

The limo slid to a stop and the engine stopped.

"We can talk about it later," she said. "Maybe after the helicopter ride."

He was more aroused than he cared to admit, and a little afraid he wasn't up to whatever she had in mind. "Remember you're not dealing with some swinging playboy."

"That's why you're so perfect for this." She smiled at him. "You're even an Eagle Scout." The limo driver opened her door and she stepped outside.

So that was her agenda, he thought. She planned to corrupt an Eagle Scout.

NATALIE HAD LOST HER NERVE, but as she strapped herself into the helicopter seat she decided everything had worked out for the best. They wouldn't have had enough time to discuss her mother's book before the helicopter ride, and doing it during the ride was totally impossible. She sat in front, next to the pilot, with Jonah directly behind her. They'd dodged the usual crowd to get to the helicopter, but once through the gate they'd been protected by a wire fence that cordoned off the landing pad.

She'd never been in a helicopter before, and her stomach tickled with excitement as she looked down through the bubble of glass that curved under her feet. Once again she reminded herself to soak up this experience—after all, she'd paid for it. The whirling blades made a lot of noise, but the pilot handed each of them a headset which provided symphony music that pretty much drowned out the heavy thumping of the rotors.

The helicopter lifted off and her stomach lurched as the ground fell away beneath her. The pilot swung the chopper out over the river, its dark surface a mirror of color and light. They glided downriver past the harbor, heading straight for the Statue of Liberty's torch. Natalie's heart pounded with anticipation as they grew closer, and closer still, until she felt as if she could touch the great lady's cheek.

After a majestic sweep around the giant statue, the pilot aimed for the financial district and the sparkling towers of the World Trade Center. He must have had a taste for drama, because as the violins swelled to a crescendo he brought them down a little and then straight up, as if they were scaling the glittering side of the building.

As they sailed up and over, headed toward Midtown, Natalie was so overcome with the beauty of it that she impulsively reached out to Jonah over the back of her seat. Instantly his hand was there, clasping hers.

They rode that way, hands linked, as the pilot soared over the distinctive scalloped lights atop the Chrysler Building and the brilliant center of Times Square. The helicopter made a tight circle above the Empire State Building while Natalie gasped at a spectacular three-hundred-sixty-degree view of the island she called home. Never had it looked more magnificent.

As the pilot reached the darker portion of the landscape that was Central Park, Natalie squeezed Jonah's hand. For better or worse, that was where this whole crazy business had started. He squeezed back.

The pilot made one more sweep over Midtown before returning to the heliport. Reluctantly, Natalie released Jonah's hand. As the rotors quieted, she took her headphones off. She was shaking with delight. She'd save her money and take this flight again. Of course, she probably wouldn't take it with Jonah. And that, she realized, might make all the difference.

She turned to the pilot. "That was amazing." She unfastened her seat belt and swiveled in her seat. "Wasn't that fantastic, Jonah?"

"Unbelievable," Jonah agreed. "Thanks."

"Glad you liked it." The pilot grinned. "I get a charge out of it myself, no matter how many times I take people up." He nodded toward a group of people just outside the fence. "Looks like your fans waited for you."

Natalie glanced at the crowd and quailed. If possible, there seemed to be more people than before. "How much would you take to fly us back out of here?" she asked, half-serious about the prospect. She didn't have much money, but she still had a credit card in her purse.

"Sorry. Can't do it," the pilot said. "The folks who

hired me would have my hide if we didn't stick to the schedule."

"We don't want to get you in trouble," Jonah said. "Let's go."

Once again in the protective curve of Jonah's arm, Natalie pushed through the mob of people and managed to get inside the limo with Jonah close behind. After the vehicle pulled away, they sat in silence for several long moments.

Finally Jonah turned to her. "Would you really like to ditch this program?"

She remembered the claustrophobia and panic she'd felt as she'd battled her way through the crowd. She thought about eating dinner at the Plaza with dozens of pairs of eyes watching every bite she took. Maybe she'd have some privacy once she was locked in her room, but then she'd be a prisoner. And the next morning she'd be living under a microscope.

"I would love to ditch this program," she said.

"That's all I needed to know." He reached out and pulled her overnight case toward them. "You'd better change into your other shoes if we're going to make a run for it."

She grinned at him. "We're literally going to run away?"

"Yep."

"Cool." She had her deck shoes on and her scarlet pumps tucked into her overnight case by the time they reached the Plaza. As a doorman approached the limo, she automatically took money for a tip out of her purse.

The car door on her side opened and the uniformed attendant held out his hand. "Welcome to the Plaza, Miss LeBlanc."

"Go ahead," Jonah said. "I'll let you know when."

"I hope you kids know what you're doing," the chauffeur said.

"Don't worry. He's an Eagle Scout," Natalie said, putting her hand in the gloved grip of the doorman.

The man gave her deck shoes a quick look of surprise before composing his features into a polite mask once again.

"It's a new fashion statement," she whispered to him.

"Of course, madam." He turned back to the limo just as Jonah climbed out with both overnight cases. "Allow me, sir."

"Sorry," Jonah said. "Can't." He glanced at Natalie. "Ready?"

"Yep."

"Then follow me!" Carrying an overnight bag in each hand, he took off in the opposite direction from the Plaza, the crowd and the gaping doorman.

Natalie thrust the tip into the man's gloved hand. "Thanks. You've been terrific," she said. Then she ran after Jonah.

He glanced back to make sure she was coming before he started across the street. "Watch out for traffic!"

She kept running. "Hey, you may be from Buffalo, but I was born here!" She could hear shouts from behind them. Somebody had sounded the alarm and people were giving chase. "Don't worry about me. Just go!"

He ran, dodging through traffic, but she could tell he was slowing his pace just for her. And he was checking on her so often he was liable to get run over.

She looked down the street and spotted an empty cab coming straight toward them. Putting her tongue to her teeth, she sent out a piercing whistle that stopped both the taxi and Jonah.

He whirled and gazed at her in astonishment. "Was that you?"

"That was me." She grinned and ran toward the cab. "Come on, before they catch us."

They opened opposite doors and jumped into the back seat, colliding with each other in the process.

"Where to?" asked the cabbie.

"Lower East Side," Jonah said, dropping the overnight cases on the floor and slamming his door. "And step on it."

The cab barely escaped the mob of people who converged on the corner.

Panting, Natalie turned to Jonah. "What's on the Lower East Side?"

He gave her a level look. "My apartment."

JONAH GAVE the driver an intersection rather than an address. He'd learned to be cautious. Fortunately his apartment building remained the one place in town where he'd be protected from the prying media and loony women who seemed constantly on his trail. From the beginning of this nightmare, the residents in the small complex had been extremely protective, misdirecting anyone who came looking for Jonah.

Natalie glanced at him in some surprise after he announced where they were going. "Not long ago, you didn't want me to know where you lived."

He still didn't know what she had in store for him, but he'd decided he'd rather face it on his own turf. "That's true. Maybe I should blindfold you."

"Maybe you should. What if I'm kidnapped by your fan club and tortured until I reveal your address? I warn you, it doesn't take much to make me sing like a canary."

He grinned, thinking how great she looked in her red dress, white furry coat and deck shoes. "I wouldn't know about that, but I can vouch for the fact that you whistle like a longshoreman."

She laughed. "Jimmy Holcomb taught me how in fifth grade. I promised never to try and kiss him again if he'd teach me how to whistle."

"I'll bet old Jimmy lived to regret that deal." He'd gotten a real kick out of that whistle, and now he enjoyed watching the laughter light up her face, making her look almost like that ten-year-old who'd chased Jimmy around the playground.

"Maybe." She gave him an impish smile. "But at the time he was desperate to get rid of me. I could run faster than he could."

"You're still pretty good at the hundred-yard dash. I wasn't sure how well you could keep up with me, but you stayed right behind."

"Oh, Jonah, wasn't that fun?"

"Yeah, it was fun." Like her, he was enjoying the high of successfully pulling off a caper, even one as small as this. Not that skipping out on the last half of the planned activities was such a crime—shoot, for the money she'd paid, she ought to be able to call the shots. Except for him, of course. She was definitely not in charge when it came to him, and in his own surroundings he could make sure of that.

He also wanted to show her his apartment to give her a dose of reality. He'd learned the hard way that being mysterious and elusive had only fired the imagination of all those women. He couldn't invite them all to his modest apartment to prove he was just a regular guy, but he could make sure Natalie knew it.

"Do you have food in this apartment of yours?" she asked.

"Absolutely." He managed to say it with conviction, but in the excitement of executing their getaway he'd forgotten all about dinner. Still, he couldn't very well drag her over there and starve her to death. He tried to remember what he had on hand. Not much. He ate a lot of meals at the station. Besides, shopping had become such a chore now, with people recognizing him left and right, that he tended to put off doing it.

"We could order up a pizza," she said.

He shook his head. "Too risky."

"You're kidding."

"Nope. I tried it once, and the first words out of the guy's mouth when I came to the door were *'You're the one who saved Bobo!'* I gave him a twenty-dollar tip and begged him to forget where I lived. I guess he kept his promise, but I'm not taking any more chances."

Natalie shook her head. "That's awful. If you can't order pizza, then you can't order anything, can you? No deli sandwiches, no Chinese, nothing."

"Actually it's not quite that bad. My neighbors took pity on me and we've worked out a system. I phone them, they phone in my order, and I pick it up from their apartment." He shrugged. "I guess if worse comes to worst, we can do that. We'll see what's in the refrigerator when we get there. Mrs. Ruggerelo keeps promising to surprise me with a batch of lasagna."

Natalie eyed him cautiously. "Who's she, your cleaning lady?"

He laughed. "Nope. Don't have one. I get to take full

credit for the state of my apartment. Mrs. Ruggerelo is a neighbor who makes outstanding lasagna."

"But you said she was going to put some in your refrigerator. How would she do that?"

"She has a key." It occurred to him that it might be a good idea if Natalie realized how chummy his apartment complex was, so she might consider modifying whatever exotic plans she had for the two of them. "In fact, about five of my neighbors have keys, I think."

"You *think?* Jonah, that sounds a little risky."

"It's the way we like it. When I'm on duty at the station, somebody checks my apartment and takes in my mail. Pete Hornacek goes upstate every other weekend to be with his grandkids, and I feed his cat. Or one of the others does, if I'm on duty that weekend. And Mrs. Sanchez is pretty old. If she has a problem, she can call from her bed and one of us can be there in no time. She doesn't have to worry about getting up to open the door."

Natalie was quiet for a while, obviously thinking about his arrangement with his neighbors. "But what if you're...involved in something personal, and Mrs. Ruggerelo decides that's the very time she's going to deliver lasagna? Couldn't that be embarrassing?"

He was glad she sounded so cautious. Maybe she wasn't quite as jaded as he'd thought. "I guess so."

"I take it you've never had something like that happen?"

"The last woman I dated liked her apartment better than mine, probably for that very reason. Come to think of it, that had a lot to do with why we broke up. She had no sense of community. She told me flat out she couldn't live like that, and I said I couldn't live any other way."

She studied him in the dim light of the cab's back seat. "So your saving my dog wasn't just an isolated case, was it?"

He sighed. "No, but I wish you wouldn't let that get around. My life is screwed up enough as it is."

The cabdriver stopped at the corner Jonah had given him. "Sure you don't want me to take you to the door?" he asked.

"Nope. This is fine," Jonah said, depositing money in the chute. "We'll get a little air." He climbed out, grabbed both bags and set them on the curb. Then he helped Natalie from the cab. Her hand felt warm and good in his.

She stepped to the sidewalk and smiled up at him. "If you're the least bit worried, you could still blindfold me. Then I wouldn't know what direction we're going and I'd never be able to find your building."

He held tight to her hand and looked into her eyes. More than anything, he wanted to kiss her right now, but he probably ought to hold off on that kind of gesture until she told him what she had in mind. His body tightened in anticipation. "You sure seem eager for that blindfold," he said. "Does that have anything to do with what you were going to ask me just before the helicopter ride?"

She looked startled. "Why, no…not at all."

He wasn't convinced. "Are you ready to tell me what this special request of yours is?"

She looked decidedly uneasy. "Um, not yet. I think we should have something to eat, don't you?"

"Okay. And after we eat you'll tell me what it is?"

"Yes." She nodded and looked very solemn. "Girl Scout's honor."

He smiled. "I thought you didn't make it past Brownies."

5

SEEING THE INSIDE of Jonah's apartment was critical to the plan, Natalie realized as they walked up two flights of stairs and approached his door. She could tell many things about him from the way he lived, and if the scheme worked, her mother would need material for describing her hero's apartment. Natalie vowed to pay close attention to details.

Unfortunately for her cool powers of observation, her heart hammered like a son of a gun as Jonah put down the overnight cases and fit the key in the lock. Inside that apartment they'd be more alone than ever before in their short acquaintance. If they could end up locked in a passionate embrace in the yacht's cabin with the crew likely to interrupt at any minute, they were in far more danger of that here.

Jonah opened the door and flipped a wall switch before gesturing for her to go in ahead of him. She stepped into a tiny hall while he picked up the overnight cases and followed her. Beyond lay his living room, and she registered a view of well-used furniture in neutral tones, a basketball balanced against a pile of books on the coffee table and a stack of magazines on the floor. Then the sound of the door closing and the lock clicking eliminated all thoughts of furniture. Except, of course, for what two people could do *on* that furniture. She wondered if she was the only one having those thoughts. Probably not.

"Can I take your coat?" His voice was very close and very husky, as if they were of a similar mind at the moment.

"Okay." As she started to take off her coat, he slipped it from her shoulders in one easy movement. *Can I take your dress? Okay.*

"This coat looks valuable." He opened the hall closet and rattled the hangers taking one out.

"Fake ermine." She hugged herself to still her trembling and walked into the living room where a single lamp cast an intimate glow. The cushions on the couch were faded but quite wide enough for…no, she mustn't think about that.

"I thought the fur was real." He closed the closet door. "But then, I wouldn't know. I've never touched real ermine, but that coat sure is soft."

She turned to face him, her pulse racing. "I…that's why I bought it."

He took off his sport coat, tossed it over the back of an easy chair and loosened his tie. She thought his fingers trembled a little, but she couldn't be sure. At any rate he looked so darned sexy that he made her dizzy.

"Want something to drink?" he asked.

"I guess." Holding a glass would give her something to do with her hands.

"Come into the kitchen and I'll see what I can offer you." Unbuttoning his cuffs, he rolled his sleeves back as he went through a doorway on his right and turned on another light.

Whatever he was offering, she was interested. There was nothing deliberately erotic about his behavior, nothing most men wouldn't do when they arrived home from a formal event. But watching Jonah get casual as he moved around his apartment was giving her way too many ideas. They hadn't planned this evening beyond their escape and finding something to eat.

Yet technically, he was hers for the weekend. If he honored that arrangement, she'd be here all night.

He opened the door of an aging refrigerator and peered inside. "I'm out of O.J." He cleared his throat. "Looks like water, cola and a fine domestic beer are the selections of the evening." He closed the refrigerator door and his gaze traveled over her red dress. When he looked into her eyes, his were filled with longing, just as they had been when she'd first appeared in the outfit. "Unfortunately you're dressed for French wine," he said, his tone gentle. "I wish I had something more exciting to offer you."

Oh, you do. But she didn't have the courage to say that. "I don't care about fancy food and drink."

"You seemed to enjoy it today on the yacht."

She shrugged. "If gourmet food's around, I figure I might as well enjoy it. But I don't eat that way all the time."

He studied her, as if he wanted to unravel the mystery of why she was so different from the way he'd pictured a woman like her to be. And he might never know, she thought, because she'd have to trust him a whole hell of a lot before she'd tell him she'd spent her retirement fund on him.

She glanced down at the cocktail dress. "I could change back into my sweatshirt and slacks, come to think of it. My shoes look dumb with the dress, and now that we're not going to eat at the Plaza, maybe I should wear something more casual."

"Don't change," he said softly.

"Why not?"

"It's like you and gourmet food. Normally I don't care about fancy clothes, but when I'm presented with something special, I can enjoy it. That's a great dress, and as for the shoes…" He grinned. "They look kind of cute."

"Oh." She met his gaze. Gradually the humor faded from his eyes as a familiar heat returned. The silence lengthened between them, and her heartbeat quickened. "Are you…that is, do you think I…were you planning on me staying…until morning?"

He leaned a shoulder against the refrigerator door. A muscle tensed in his jaw. "Are you planning to stay?"

"I…don't know." She swallowed the nervous lump in her throat. "The hotel arrangements were less personal. It wasn't like I was paying for the privilege of spending the night with you, but now that's exactly what it feels like."

"Are you telling me I have the right to say no to your advances and put you in a cab after dinner?"

She wasn't sure what she was saying. She needed a certain amount of time to gracefully lead up to her mother's book idea, but the more hours she spent with him the more trouble she'd have sticking to her original plan. There were some occasions in a girl's life when she didn't want to be reminded of her mother. Being alone with Jonah in this apartment certainly qualified.

"If I sent you home early tonight, it wouldn't seem that you'd gotten your money's worth," he said. It sounded suave, but a little hitch in his voice gave away his own nervousness.

Her insides felt all quivery with anticipation. She

couldn't even take offense at his passing reference to the money she'd paid. "I guess not."

"Don't worry. I'm way too curious about this request of yours to send you home until after I've heard it."

"Oh." Okay, so *he'd* take care of reminding her of her mother. That lifted some of the responsibility off her shoulders. "That's good. Then let's have a beer."

"And discuss your request?" he asked casually, opening the refrigerator again.

"Maybe. Do you have peanuts?"

He peered around the edge of the door, frowning. "What on God's green earth would you do with peanuts?"

She stared at him in total confusion. "I thought—now, this is just a suggestion, so feel free to veto it—but I thought we could eat them."

"Oh."

"What did *you* think I meant?"

He shook his head. "Never mind. And yes, I have peanuts. Unfortunately there isn't much else around here, though." He took two bottles of beer out of the refrigerator and closed it. "Mrs. Ruggerelo didn't come over today with lasagna."

"We had a big lunch. I don't need much to eat tonight, anyway."

"Good thing." Carrying the bottles by the neck in one hand, he walked over to a small pantry and took out a can of peanuts. "Glasses are in the cupboard next to the sink, if you wouldn't mind getting them down."

"Sure." She opened the cupboard and took out two glasses. There were no dirty dishes in the sink, she noticed. Her mother would like hearing about that. Dirty dishes probably wouldn't fit her image of a hero.

In fact, Jonah would get all sorts of approval ratings from her mother, Natalie thought as they settled on the couch. He was close enough to increase her pulse rate considerably. She watched the flex of his forearm as he twisted the cap off the first bottle and she stared at him pouring beer into the glass as if she'd never seen anyone do it before. He had such competent hands, such nice fingers. She noticed a light patch of skin about the size of a silver dollar on his wrist.

He handed her the foaming glass of beer. "Did you think I'd spill it?"

"No!" She was blushing again. "I just…wondered where you got that scar on your wrist."

He looked at it as if he'd forgotten all about having it. Then he started pouring the second beer. "My glove pulled away during a fire, about…let's see, I guess it was about four years ago."

She didn't like hearing that. It made her shudder to think of all the hundreds of times he'd chopped his way into burning buildings. "Have you been hurt often?"

"Nope, fortunately."

"How many times?" His aftershave teased her, making her want to snuggle closer, but she restrained herself. They probably should talk about her mother's book. This was the perfect time, relaxing with a drink on his couch, side by side…. She'd just have to ignore that little ache growing deep within her.

He finished pouring the beer and tapped his glass to hers. "Cheers."

"Cheers." She took a sip. "And you didn't answer my question. How many times have you been hurt?"

"I don't know. I haven't kept count." He took a

drink of beer. "Most of it was little stuff, like this burn on my wrist. It's nothing."

She was a glutton for punishment. She didn't want to hear it, but she desperately wanted to know. "Most?"

"I've only been in the hospital once, and that was for smoke inhalation when my mask came off. I guess there's some scarring in my lungs. Want some peanuts?"

Her heart squeezed at his offhand attitude about his injuries. She hated the idea that he pulled a mask over that wonderful face and plunged into hell several times a week. She wanted to demand he stop putting himself in jeopardy. But that was stupid and she didn't have any right to, anyway. She took a handful of the shelled nuts from the can. "What do your parents think of the danger you're in all the time?"

"Oh, they pretty much hate it. But this is what I've wanted to do ever since I was six years old." He tossed a peanut into his mouth.

She watched him chew and enjoyed the way it made his dimples flash in his cheeks. She also thought about what his mouth had felt like on hers, and how much she wanted to have that experience again. It would be wonderful, and also reassuring after all this discussion of peril. "Do you like your job because of the excitement?"

"Some of it's that." He gazed at her, his dark eyes taking on the same sort of heat they had when they'd been alone in the yacht's cabin. "But mostly because it's so morally simple. When you fight fire, you have no doubt who the enemy is. You can fight it...with everything you've got."

He framed her face with both hands. "Let's stop talking about fires and superheroes."

His touch made her vibrate, and her voice became breathy with excitement. "What do you want to talk about?"

"I don't want to talk at all."

As he took possession of her mouth and urged her down against the cushions of the worn couch, the wonder of having him kiss her again pushed everything from her mind but the mastery of his lips, the eloquent suggestion of his tongue and the heavenly weight of his body on hers. She responded with absolute surrender. As he trailed kisses down her throat to the low-cut bodice of her dress, the peanuts she'd been holding dribbled slowly out of her open hand onto the carpet.

A key rattled in the front-door lock.

"Damn, I forgot the chain." Jonah leaped from the couch and started for the door.

Natalie sat up quickly and adjusted her dress. Shoot, how had she allowed herself to get horizontal so fast? And wasn't Jonah supposed to be reminding her of her request instead of kissing her senseless?

"Jonah, you're here!" cried a woman as the door opened.

"Hello, Mrs. Ruggerelo."

I've been saved by the lasagna lady, Natalie thought.

HE SHOULD HAVE PUT the chain on, Jonah thought, deeply regretting the interruption. He never did use the chain, but considering what had been developing on the couch just now, the chain would have been a very good idea.

"I thought you'd be at the Plaza tonight living it up with that crazy rich woman, my little bambino," said

Mrs. Ruggerelo as she balanced a covered dish in both hands. At four foot eleven she had to crane her neck to look up at Jonah. "So what happened?"

Jonah winced and hoped Natalie hadn't heard that description of her. He also hoped the dimness of the hall disguised the bulge in his pants, and that he'd wiped all Natalie's lipstick off his mouth.

"We changed our plans," he said, blocking the hallway. "Do I smell lasagna?"

"Now what else would I have in here, old gym socks? Of course you smell lasagna. What do you mean, *we*?"

"The crazy rich woman decided the Plaza was no fun," Natalie said from behind him.

Jonah turned and tried to think how he could smooth over the awkwardness of Mrs. Ruggerelo's remark.

Natalie took the opportunity to duck around him. She smiled at Jonah's neighbor. "You couldn't have better timing, Mrs. Ruggerelo. We're starved."

Mrs. Ruggerelo, who was nearly as round as she was tall, almost dropped the covered dish she was carrying. "It's you! Bobo's mother!"

Jonah groaned.

Natalie, however, seemed delighted with being called Bobo's mother. "He is sort of like my little kid. Puppies get under your skin, you know."

"I know they do. I loved our little Tootsie, but after she died, Leo said no more dogs. Still, when I saw Jonah with that puppy, I started wishing for one again. And you know what? There are no more little black puppies of any kind at the animal shelters!"

"Really? Why that's wonderful!"

Jonah stared at the two women in disbelief. He'd

never seen such an instant bond in his life. He hoped the chitchat would be over soon. He wanted to do some bonding of his own with Natalie on the couch.

"Jonah's told me so much about your lasagna," Natalie said. "I can hardly wait."

"Me, neither," Jonah said without enthusiasm. Natalie was being a good sport, though. If he was any judge, she'd been ready to rip his clothes off a few minutes ago, and now she was acting as if Mrs. Ruggerelo was the very person she wanted to see. She was probably just being considerate after the way he'd raved about his neighbors. Which was sweet, but he'd had enough of the chumminess.

Time to take command of the situation, he decided. "Why don't I take that dish, Mrs. Ruggerelo, so you can be on your way? I'm sure Mr. Ruggerelo is expecting you to come right back." He reached for the lasagna.

Mrs. Ruggerelo pulled it out of reach. Meanwhile, she was very busy inspecting Natalie from top to toe. "Interesting choice of shoes."

"We had to run," Natalie said.

"I'll tell you all about it next time I see you." Jonah reached for the dish again.

Mrs. Ruggerelo drew back. "It's not hot enough to eat. I was planning to pop it in your refrigerator for you to have tomorrow night."

"So we'll warm it up." Jonah made another grab for the dish.

Mrs. Ruggerelo stepped into the hall, taking the lasagna with her. "I have a better idea." She gave Natalie one more glance and nodded, as if coming to a conclusion. "I'll bet you don't eat proper food. You're like all young girls nowadays, thin as a fettuccine noodle.

Come with me." She started down the hall carrying her lasagna. "I'll feed you both a fine Italian dinner. I have bread, antipasto, wine."

"That sounds terrific," Natalie said, walking after her.

Jonah caught her arm and drew her back. Natalie was carrying this neighborly attitude a little too far. "It does sound terrific, for another night. Wednesday. Wednesday's good for me. Natalie?"

"I think tonight sounds fine."

"But..." He paused. He couldn't very well tell her why he wanted to postpone the invitation, not when Mrs. R. was all ears.

Mrs. Ruggerelo turned back to them. "You have to eat, and I know there's nothing in your refrigerator. What were you planning to feed this girl, peanuts?"

Natalie glanced up at Jonah, an unreadable smile on her face.

"We'll manage," he said, trying to decipher the look in Natalie's eyes. "We had a big lunch, right, Natalie?"

"I know." Mrs. Ruggerelo smiled, revealing one gold tooth. "I saw you on the news tonight squeezing her around the middle, doing that rescue thing when somebody's choking to death."

"Aw, jeez." Jonah passed a hand over his face and looked at his neighbor. "It was really on the news?"

"If you ran away from the Plaza, that will probably be on the ten o'clock news." Mrs. Ruggerelo winked. "You might have to go to work wearing my old hat and Leo's raggedy coat, like you did after you saved Bobo."

Natalie grinned as she glanced at him. "You failed to mention that."

"Yeah, well, it's not a picture I like to dwell on." Jonah had gone to the station that day looking like a tall bag lady or a seedy transvestite. The guys had used both descriptions. In any city other than New York, he never would have gotten away with it.

"It worked," Mrs. Ruggerelo said. "Nobody's traced you to this apartment house yet. So, are you coming for dinner or what?"

"Sure," Natalie said.

Jonah was extremely confused. He hadn't imagined that moan of delight when he'd kissed her, so why wasn't she as eager to get rid of this unwelcome visitor as he was? "Look, Mrs. Ruggerelo, if you'd be willing to just order us a pizza, I'll pick it up from your place. I don't want you going to all this trouble, considering you like to turn in early, and—"

"Are you kidding?" the plump little woman said. "I wouldn't miss the ten o'clock news tonight for anything. I want to see how you two made a break for it. Come on down to my apartment for a decent meal. You can have pizza anytime."

"Not with the toppings I had in mind," Jonah muttered low enough that only Natalie heard him. He gave her a significant glance, but she merely looked innocent, as if she had no idea what he was talking about.

"Besides," Mrs. Ruggerelo continued, "Leo spilled tomato soup at lunch today and it spread under the recliner. I can't budge it to clean the rug, and if somebody doesn't move it soon, Leo will try. You know how long he was laid up the last time. I was going to write you a note about it when I left the lasagna. I was afraid I wouldn't get the stain out if it sat overnight, but I thought I didn't have a choice. However, now that you—"

"Okay." Jonah sighed. He couldn't fight both

women, and apparently Natalie no longer wanted to be alone with him. Maybe his first assessment was right, and she was crazy, after all. Most normal women couldn't be fiery hot one minute and cool as a cucumber the next. If that was the case with Natalie, he'd better use some caution tonight. "We'd love to have dinner at your place."

6

MRS. RUGGERELO REMINDED Natalie of her mother, although the two women looked nothing alike. The minute she stepped into the Ruggerelo's apartment, she understood. They shared the same attitude—benevolent bossiness. Natalie's decision to bid on Jonah had brought back her mother's familiar meddling behavior, replacing the hopeless inactivity of depression.

The Ruggerelos' apartment was as cozy as her parents' place used to be, making her nostalgic for the days when her father had been alive. People who could stick out a marriage for thirty-plus years should be rewarded by being allowed to grow old together, she thought. She missed her father terribly.

"Look who we have here, Leo!" Mrs. Ruggerelo announced as she breezed into the apartment and set her lasagna on top of the television cabinet.

Leo Ruggerelo looked up from his program with a start, and his recliner footrest came down with a thump as he hauled himself to his feet. "Jonah? What the hell? Oh, excuse me, ma'am." He peered at Natalie over the tops of his glasses. "Well, damned if it's not the puppy woman!"

"In the flesh. Miss Natalie LeBlanc." Mrs. Ruggerelo sounded as if she was introducing royalty. With practiced ease she scooped up the remote and flicked off the television. "I've invited them for dinner."

Leo looked confused. "But we already had—"

"We'll sit with them and make pleasant conversation." She gave her husband a commanding look that made Natalie smile. Her mother had sent her father that sort of look more times than Natalie could count. Although her father had dominated in intellectual matters, Alice had been in charge of the social graces.

"Oh. Sure, sure." Leo glanced at Jonah. "Say, now that you're here, maybe you could give me a hand moving the recliner. Spilled some soup today."

"Be glad to."

"Natalie and I will take care of things in the kitchen while you two handle that little chore." Mrs. Ruggerelo picked up her casserole again. "You know where the stain remover is, Leo. Come on, Natalie."

A moment later Natalie was spreading sliced bread with garlic butter while Mrs. Ruggerelo made the antipasto.

"Everybody's been curious about you," Mrs. Ruggerelo said. "We all think Jonah's wonderful, of course, but that was a lot of money you paid."

"I guess it seems frivolous to you." Natalie was having more and more trouble with the role of capricious rich girl. She decided to trust this woman with at least part of the truth. "I did it for my mother."

Mrs. Ruggerelo whirled, her hand on her heart. "You bought him for your *mother?*"

Natalie flushed. "Not the way you're thinking. You see, she's been depressed ever since my father died, but she was so taken with the image of Jonah rescuing Bobo. I thought if I—"

"Say no more." Mrs. Ruggerelo reached over and patted Natalie's arm. "You thought if she saw you with a fine young man on your arm, she'd take more interest in the future." Mrs. Ruggerelo's dark eyes glowed. "What a considerate daughter you are, thinking of your mother like that." She went back to chopping.

Natalie felt a little better.

"My two girls, they would do that for me, bless their hearts, although they don't have your kind of money, of course. Fortunately they both have nice young men, and last year I became the grandmother of a perfect little boy."

"I'll bet you love that."

Mrs. Ruggerelo nodded. "So will your mother. The only way you can cheat death of its hold is to think about birth."

Natalie wasn't sure how they'd leaped from dating to pregnancy. "I wasn't really planning that far ahead. I mean, Jonah and I barely know each other."

The round little woman began to quiver with laughter.

"What?"

"I think you know each other well enough. When I opened the door, Jonah—well, I don't think he was smuggling zucchini, if you know what I mean."

Natalie figured she'd just turned the color of her dress.

Mrs. Ruggerelo pretended not to notice Natalie's embarrassment as she continued assembling the antipasto. "Did you come here for dinner to stall him off?"

Natalie opened her mouth to speak but nothing came out.

"Maybe you want to keep him guessing, and I can understand that. Paying all that money puts a girl in an awkward position. She looks pretty desperate."

Natalie managed a small murmur of agreement.

Mrs. Ruggerelo glanced up from her work. "But if I

were you, I wouldn't play too many games with this boy. You want him, you just go get him. Make lots of babies and give your mother joy."

Natalie swallowed. "I...hadn't even considered... babies."

The older woman's eyes twinkled. "Oh, of course you have. You might not know it yet, because of all the commotion." She waved both hands in the air. "Such elaborate schemes young people cook up these days. Video dating, singles bars, bachelor auctions. It all boils down to one thing—finding a mate and making babies."

"But not everyone—"

"Of course not everyone has babies, and some shouldn't have them. But that's what the equipment was designed for, when you get right down to it."

"What equipment?" Jonah asked, coming into the kitchen. He glanced at Natalie. "Are you okay?"

She took a deep breath and made a conscious effort not to let her gaze wander lower than his face. "I'm fine."

"Girl talk," Mrs. Ruggerelo said, flashing her gold tooth. "And now the food is ready!"

JONAH ENJOYED the meal, but he couldn't help watching the clock. This whole weekend had a Cinderella feel to it, and any minute he expected Natalie to disappear into the night, never to be seen again. He should be relieved to see her go, with all her unpredictable behavior and wild spending habits, not to mention whatever kinky request she planned to make of him.

Yet the longer he was with her, alone or in the company of other people, the more fascinated he became.

The Ruggerelos treated her like one of their daughters, and she seemed to soak up the easy affection. He liked watching her laugh and have a good time. He just thought they could be having a much better time by themselves.

Funny how he and Cynthia had broken up because she resented how close he was to his neighbors. Now the tables were turned and Natalie seemed to love that closeness, while he was the one who wanted more privacy.

Of course the situation was completely different with Natalie. He'd been thinking of asking Cynthia to marry him, so her reaction to his neighbors was important. In this case, Natalie's reaction didn't matter, because he couldn't imagine having a serious relationship with someone who'd spend thirty-three thousand dollars at a bachelor auction. Still, he wouldn't mind being alone with her for the rest of the night. If nothing else, he was dying of curiosity about her mysterious request. But she seemed to prefer schmoozing with the neighbors.

"I can't imagine a better meal than this at the Plaza," Natalie said, polishing off her second helping of lasagna.

"Well, there is something about home-cooked," Mrs. Ruggerelo said, beaming.

Jonah figured Natalie was now an honorary member of the family after praising Mrs. R.'s cooking like that. In fact, he'd better say something nice or risk being in the doghouse. "It was great," he said.

Mrs. Ruggerelo arched her eyebrows. "Better than pizza in a cardboard box?"

"Much better," Jonah said. "I don't know what I was thinking."

"I do," she said with a tiny smile.

A ringing phone saved Jonah from making any comment, but he was sure he was blushing as Leo excused himself to go answer the phone.

While Leo was gone, Natalie lobbed in another sure-fire compliment. "Do you ever give out your recipes?" she asked.

"Only to certain people." Her expression filled with pride, Mrs. Ruggerelo adjusted the alignment of the empty lasagna dish on a decorative hot pad. "I would give it to you." She paused. "And you could share it with your mother, if you want."

"That would be fantastic. But I don't cook much. You might have to coach me the first time."

"Just call."

Jonah watched the give-and-take between the two women with great interest. They'd formed a friendship, one that seemed likely to last beyond this weekend. Hell, he hadn't even crossed that particular bridge, and Mrs. R. was already standing happily on the other side.

Leo came back, his tone full of apology. "Jonah, that was Mrs. Sanchez. I'm afraid you're the only one who can help her."

Jonah got to his feet immediately, a stab of fear going through him. "What's wrong?"

"Nothing terrible. She was doing fine tonight until she got one of her dizzy spells and had to sit in her easy chair. She doesn't want to spend the night in the chair, but every time she stands up she gets dizzy again, and she's afraid she might fall."

"Should we call the paramedics?"

"I don't think so." Leo smiled. "If you want to know the truth, I think she heard you were back in the building and she's dying to find out what happened with your weekend. She mentioned that Pete Hornacek saw you come in and gave her a call. She tried your apartment and then called here when you didn't answer."

"Just go carry her into her bedroom and make sure she's taken her pills," said Mrs. Ruggerelo. "That will make her happy as a lark. Then you can come back here for zabaglione."

Jonah recognized a bribe when he heard one. Mrs. R. knew good and well that the sweet Italian pudding, especially her version, had become his favorite dessert. But it wasn't as tempting as being alone again with Natalie.

Natalie pushed back her chair. "I'll go with you to see Mrs. Sanchez."

Jonah started to tell her to stay here, but thought better of it. This interruption of Mrs. Sanchez's could be their ticket out of the Ruggerelos' friendly apartment. With the way Natalie was settling in here, if they came back for dessert, they might end up staying until midnight playing cribbage or some damn thing.

"You make the best zabaglione on the planet, Mrs. R.," he said, "but I'm stuffed. Could we take a rain check?" He glanced at Natalie to see if she'd back him on this move.

"I'm pretty full, too," Natalie said, her color high. "Although it does sound wonderful."

Hot damn, Jonah thought.

"I'll send it with you, then," said Mrs. Ruggerelo. She winked at Natalie. "You might have more of an appetite later."

"I'll clear some dishes while you package it up," Natalie said, suddenly very busy avoiding Jonah's gaze. Then she whisked into the kitchen after Mrs.

Ruggerelo, leaving Jonah standing in the dining room with Leo.

Leo watched Natalie until she was out of sight before turning to Jonah. He motioned him into the living room, and when they got there he lowered his voice. "Did you find out if anything's wrong with her or not?"

"Such as?"

"You know." Leo twirled his finger beside his temple. "Nuts."

Jonah wasn't about to tell Leo about his suspicions regarding Natalie's special request, so he shrugged. "She seems pretty normal to me."

"Jonah, the woman's wearing deck shoes with a cocktail dress. Doesn't that give you a clue?"

Jonah grinned. "I told her to do that so we could escape from the Plaza. I think it looks kind of cute."

"You like her, don'tcha? I've been watching you, and you like her."

"Well, so far, yeah. I mean, what's not to like?" And there was a hell of a lot to like, he added to himself.

"Okay, she's a looker, and polite and all. I can see how you'd be attracted, but you gotta be careful."

It was reasonable advice, Jonah knew, the sort of thing he'd been telling himself ever since the night of the bachelor auction. He just had trouble following it whenever Natalie came within kissing distance.

"No offense," Leo continued, "but would a normal woman pay thirty-three grand to go out with a guy, even a stud like you? I can understand a few hundred bucks, seein' as how it was for a good cause, maybe even a thousand if you needed the income-tax deduction. But this is some deduction."

"I know." Jonah rubbed the back of his neck. "I can't

figure it out, either. She doesn't act like someone who throws money around for no reason."

"Did she make a pass?"

Jonah smiled grimly. "Nope. But I did."

"Well, I can't blame you, but the whole thing makes me nervous. What happened?"

"Mrs. R. showed up."

That made Leo chuckle. "She has a sixth sense about things like that. Used to drive the girls crazy. They'd be making out with some guy on the couch, trying to be quiet. Me, I'd be dead to the world, but she'd wake up and go out there with milk and cookies." He glanced toward the kitchen. "She likes Natalie."

"I noticed."

"That's another strange thing. She's usually a pretty good judge of character."

"After all, she agreed to marry you," Jonah said with a grin.

"Damn straight."

Jonah hesitated. "How long did you know Mrs. R. before you decided she was the one?"

Leo's gaze was steady. "I didn't know her at all. I just saw her at a party, and something clicked. Oh, we went through all the motions—dating, meeting the families, talking about the future, but I'd pretty much made up my mind the first time I laid eyes on her." He paused. "I wasn't wrong."

"Obviously not."

Leo rubbed his chin as he studied Jonah. "You told me that you saw Natalie in the park lots of times before her dog went in the drink. You were going to ask her out, you said. Did something click for you, too?"

"I thought so. But then after the auction, I figured I

was wrong. Like you said, what normal woman would pay out thirty-three grand like that?"

Leo nodded. "Yeah, that would throw up the yellow caution flags for me, too. I'd hate to see you get into some fatal-attraction thing where somebody boiled your bunny in a soup pot."

"I don't have a bunny."

Leo clapped him on the back. "Good point. But keep your eyes open, okay? There's something fishy going on. I don't know what it is yet, but that Natalie doesn't have all her cards on the table."

NATALIE HELD the zabaglione as they stood outside Mrs. Sanchez's door, and Jonah rapped softly. They'd decided not to make a trip back to the apartment to drop off the dessert when Mrs. Sanchez might need Jonah right away.

For sure Natalie needed him. The time spent with the Ruggerelos hadn't helped one darn bit to control her fascination with him. In fact, it seemed to have made things worse. His voice, his low chuckle and his teasing glance had all sharpened her hunger almost past enduring.

But it was plain old-fashioned lust, not some subliminal desire to mate and have babies. She'd be willing to bet on that. Someday she might think about marrying. After she and her husband had a chance to settle in, they might consider a baby. But that was years away. Mrs. Ruggerelo didn't understand that times had changed, and women didn't feel the same biological rush they used to back in her day.

"She might have fallen asleep," Jonah said. He rapped a little harder.

"Come in, Jonah," called a gentle voice from the other side of the door.

Jonah used his key to open the door. "Mrs. Sanchez? I brought a friend."

"How wonderful. Come right in, *mihito*, and introduce your friend."

Natalie followed Jonah into the apartment, where the exotic scent of peppers spiced the air.

"Mrs. Sanchez," Jonah said, "may I present Natalie LeBlanc."

"The puppy lady?" A frail-looking woman with gray hair sat in a huge easy chair that dwarfed her. "Come closer," she said, beckoning with both hands. "I can't remember where I put my glasses, and my eyes, they aren't so good anymore. Let me see you, Natalie LeBlanc."

Natalie walked up to the chair. "I'm glad to meet you, Mrs. Sanchez." She cradled the container of zabaglione against her body so she could reach down and shake the woman's hand. The lid slipped, and before she knew it, she'd slopped the pale yellow dessert down the side of her dress. "Aw, shoot!" She held the container away from her and ran her finger up the sides to catch the drips before they ended up on Mrs. Sanchez or the carpet.

"Give me the dish," Jonah said, taking it out of her hand. "And don't move. I'll get something to clean that with." He headed toward the back of the apartment.

"Too bad," Mrs. Sanchez said. "And your dress is *muy bonita*. Is that Mrs. Ruggerelo's zabaglione?"

"Yep." Natalie started licking the dessert off her fingers. "And it's delicious."

"Will your dress be all right?"

"I hope so." She wondered if the cleaners would be

able to salvage it. She'd spent hours going through the sales racks to find it and had been proud of her guerrilla-shopping techniques. Besides that, the dress would always be linked with thoughts of Jonah. No matter what happened between them, she wanted to be able to savor the memories the garment had already collected.

Jonah returned while Natalie was still licking her fingers. She hadn't meant the action to be provocative, but judging from Jonah's intense glance as he handed her the damp dishcloth, it was extremely provocative. "Do you need..." He stopped to clear his throat. "Any help?"

"Not this time, thanks," she said, her heart hammering as she met his heated gaze. Wow. It was a wonder the room hadn't burst into flames. She had to break this spell or Mrs. Sanchez would notice. She glanced away and began dabbing at the zabaglione on her dress. "But you must be getting tired of constantly having to save me."

Mrs. Sanchez chuckled. "Jonah doesn't get tired of saving people, do you, *mihito?*"

"What?" he murmured, still looking at Natalie.

"You're born to rescue people," Mrs. Sanchez said. "I get dizzy, you come right away to carry me to my bed." She reached up and patted Jonah's arm. "Just like they say on TV. A hero."

Jonah sighed. "No, I'm not, Mrs. Sanchez. That's just a lot of media hype. I thought at least the people in this building would—"

"The people in this building *especially* know it's true," Mrs. Sanchez said. "You fix things when the super can't get to it, you run errands...well, you used to run errands until women started chasing you down the street."

Natalie glanced up. "They did? When?"

Mrs. Sanchez laughed, a high, tinkling sound. "I saw him from my window with two big bags full of diapers for poor Mrs. Sullivan—she has triplets and her husband's working overtime to make ends meet. They never have a chance to get everything done. Everybody tries to help. I've crocheted baby things, which is all I can do, but Jonah's done the most."

"Not really," Jonah protested. "Just yesterday the Jansens—"

"Oh, *mihito*, you do the most, so just be quiet and let me tell the story. So he had two big bags stuffed, and I hear someone shout, '*It's him!*' I look out my window, and see two ladies chasing him like crazy. I cried out '*Andale, andale!*' But he couldn't hear me. He had to take quite a detour, but he outlasted them and didn't lose any of those diapers, either. Good thing he's in shape."

"It's ridiculous what's happened since that puppy thing," Jonah said, his face slightly red. "I just hope it's over soon."

Natalie wasn't so much intrigued by the idea of women running after Jonah as she was by the thought of him going out to buy extra diapers for a frantic mother of triplets. She had a sudden picture of him buying diapers for his own children. The mental image was probably Mrs. Ruggerelo's fault, what with all her harping on the subject of mating and babies. But even so, the concept of Jonah as a father was a riveting one.

Her chest tightened with unfamiliar longing as she pictured Jonah swinging a small child up on his broad shoulders to watch the Macy's parade, or reaching out his large hand to a much smaller one as he walked with his son or daughter through the Central Park Zoo. Then she had another thought, one that bothered her more than she wanted to admit.

She wondered what lucky woman would be holding the child's other hand.

7

JONAH WASN'T CRAZY about standing there while Mrs. Sanchez sang his praises, but he liked the way Natalie was looking at him as a result—so gentle and sweet, as if she had the urge to kiss him. When she gave him that sort of sentimental look, he had a hard time thinking of her as some jaded rich chick.

Maybe she'd had ulterior motives and kinky plans when she'd bid on him. Maybe before the night was over he'd find out that this woman was totally unbalanced and capable of all sorts of strange behavior. But damned if he could believe it right this minute. Then again, his mother had always told him he was gullible.

"Well, I'm sure you two young people want to get on with your evening," Mrs. Sanchez said. "If you'd just carry me into my bedroom, Jonah, I'll be out of your way."

"Sure thing," Jonah said, leaning down to slip his arms under the tiny woman.

"Wait," Natalie said. "Why don't we all share Mrs. Ruggerelo's zabaglione before we go?"

Joy suffused the old woman's face, and Jonah felt like a selfish heel for wishing Natalie hadn't come up with the idea. He loved making his neighbors happy, but in this case making Mrs. Sanchez happy would delay being alone with Natalie.

"I wouldn't want to intrude," Mrs. Sanchez said shyly.

"You wouldn't be intruding." Jonah settled her back into the chair. "Natalie and I will go dish some out for all three of us. How's that?"

"Oh." Her dark eyes sparkled. "That would be special."

"Be right back." Jonah grabbed Natalie's hand and led her toward Mrs. Sanchez's small kitchen.

"I hope you don't mind," she murmured after they were out of earshot. "But she seems so lonely, and—"

Jonah pulled her into the kitchen, keeping a firm grip on her hand. "Of course I don't mind," he said. "It's the right thing to do." He cradled her head in his other hand. "And so's this." He took her ripe mouth, flavored with zabaglione, and wondered if he'd made a mistake by kissing her. She was so luscious, so ready to kiss him back, that he might not have the will to let her go.

Apparently she was the one with the willpower. When he let go of her hand to draw her in tight against him, she wouldn't budge. It didn't make sense. She was kissing him as if she couldn't get enough, yet she was struggling to keep distance between her body and his. He had the strength to overrule her, but that wasn't his way.

He lifted his mouth a fraction from hers and gulped for air as he urged her closer. "Stop wiggling and come here."

"No." She was as breathless as he was.

"Why not?"

"My dress is all icky with zabaglione. You'll get it on your clothes."

His low laugh was filled with frustration. "To hell

with that." Once he put some muscle into it she was no match for him. He absorbed her gasp of surprise as he lowered his mouth to hers once again. If she'd been responsive before, she was wild for him now, digging her fingers into his shoulder muscles. He moaned with pleasure at how perfectly her body aligned with his, as if that had been the original plan for both of them.

He lost track of whether the rapid heartbeat belonged to him or to her, or if the frantic drumming was identical as they strained against each other. In no time he was hard and aching. Knowing he couldn't take much of this torture, he forced himself to ease back, lifting his mouth so he could just barely nibble at her lips. His shirt pulled a little, sticking to the goo on her dress.

"See?" she whispered.

It was the huskiest, sexiest voice he'd ever had the pleasure of hearing at a moment like this. He wished he could see…everything. "I was hoping the stuff would glue us together permanently," he murmured, looking into her eyes.

"No such luck." Her expression was dreamy as she slowly withdrew from his arms. "We'd better get the dessert ready."

"Guess so." He released her with great regret. "The sooner we do that, the sooner we can make our excuses and leave."

"Jonah…" Her cheeks became rosier than ever. "We need to talk."

"About your request?"

She nodded.

"We will," he said. But he didn't think he wanted to hear it. He was afraid to burst this bubble by finding out about some elaborate scheme that might suck the romance right out of this night. He took a long, steadying breath and walked over to a cupboard. "I'll get the bowls and dish the stuff out. Silverware's in the drawer next to the stove."

"You really do know your way around your neighbors' apartments, don't you?"

"I should." He divided the zabaglione in three equal portions. "I've lived here almost five years."

"I've lived in my apartment building almost all my life, and the only other apartment I know this well is my mother's."

He paused in the act of scraping the bowl. This was new information. "Your mother lives in that building, too?"

"Um, yes." She rattled the silverware as she grabbed it from the drawer.

He wondered if it was his imagination or if mention of her mother had been a little slip on her part. He rinsed the zabaglione bowl and took a tray from a bottom cupboard before he asked the next question, not wanting her to think he was grilling her. Keeping his back to her, he set the bowls on the tray. "Does she know about this bachelor auction?" he asked as casually as possible.

"I think the entire city knows. There was that big article in the *Times.*"

Still he didn't turn around. "So what did she say about it?"

In the silence Natalie cleared her throat. "Um…she understands," she finally replied.

Well, that makes two of you, but I'm still in the dark. He imagined his own mother's reaction if she'd picked up the Buffalo paper and found out he'd done something like that, or even remotely like that. Both she and his father would have gone ballistic. But apparently Natalie's mother *understood* her daughter's reasons for spending thirty-three thousand on a weekend with a guy. Maybe it was only pin money in the LeBlanc family. If so he was way out of his league, and he'd better remember it.

He picked up the tray and turned toward her. Judging from her expression, she was definitely hiding something from him. Just as Leo had said, Natalie didn't have all her cards on the table.

He angled his head toward the living room. "Let's go have dessert."

THIS WHOLE SCHEME was getting more complicated by the minute, Natalie thought as she perched on the couch and ate her bowl of zabaglione. She hadn't counted on this uncontrollable passion. When Jonah had kissed her moments ago, her brain had short-circuited. It was amazing that she'd even remembered the glop on her dress and tried to keep it off him.

And as if his kiss hadn't been enough to turn her into mush, he'd thrown in that macho strong-arm stuff. Me, Tarzan, you, Jane. It still worked, even in this enlightened age, she thought in wonder. God, she'd loved the way he'd laughed and hauled her against him. She could still feel the sensation of his muscles bunching and the moment of contact with his aroused body. He'd set her on fire, and tendrils of heat continued to spread through her as she relived it.

She wanted him to drag her by the hair back to his apartment. She wanted him to push her to the floor and have his way with her without asking permission. Very primitive. Very satisfying. Very unwise. She hadn't so much as hinted at her mother's book idea.

She'd hoped that during the evening they'd become good enough friends that she could tell him her reason for bidding on him. They could treat the whole experience as something of a lark and even laugh together about her inventiveness. Then he'd agree to help, and her mission would be accomplished.

Unfortunately, now that she knew him better, she didn't believe he'd react that way at all. If he was uncomfortable with Mrs. Sanchez's tales about him, he would probably hate the idea of being the inspiration for a romance hero. He was operating on the assumption that she'd bid on him for her own reasons, reasons involving sexual attraction. Natalie knew that was part of what excited him and motivated his desire for her. What would happen to all that excitement if he learned she'd begun this venture as a business deal?

For one unworthy minute she considered not telling him about the book. If she allowed their relationship to develop naturally and introduced him to her mother in due time, Alice would get what she needed from him eventually.

Only two people in the world knew Natalie's true motivation, herself and her friend Barb, and Barb would never give her away. But as Natalie watched Jonah talking and laughing with Mrs. Sanchez, as she remembered that he'd acted with honesty from the beginning, she realized she could do no less for him. He deserved the truth, and he deserved it quickly.

She'd tell him the minute they got back to his apartment, before he kissed her again and made her lose her resolve, not to mention all her clothes. Once she started kissing him, no matter where they happened to be, she wanted it to go on forever. She'd never enjoyed kissing a man this much. She'd like to make it her new hobby.

He glanced over at her, as if reading her thoughts. "I think it's about time for us to go," he said. There was an unmistakable light of anticipation in his eyes.

Her pulse quickened. If only this were a simpler evening and they could return to the apartment and pick up where they left off. But she couldn't allow that. Not yet. "You're right. We have some things to discuss."

His answering smile indicated that he didn't think they'd spend much time on discussion. "Right." He stood. "I'll rinse out these dishes and then—"

Mrs. Sanchez's doorbell chimed.

The tiny woman clapped her hands together. "*Bueno!* More company! This night has been a busy one."

"You could say that." Jonah put down the tray and went to answer the door. "Hey, Pete," he said to the person in the hallway. "What's up?"

With Jonah filling most of the doorway, Natalie could barely see the short, stocky person standing there, but she figured out it had to be Pete Hornacek, the man with the cat.

"Hate to bother you, Jonah," he said, "but the Sullivans' sink is stopped up again. I can't seem to find my plunger, and Beth doesn't know where anything is in their apartment these days. Sully's working the late shift, and she needs help." He tried to peer around Jonah. "I went to see if the Ruggerelos had one, but they loaned theirs to their daughter, and they said to try you down here at Mrs. Sanchez's place."

Natalie was beginning to believe she'd stumbled into a commune. Jonah had encountered more of his neighbors in one night than she did in a month.

"No problem," Jonah said. "Just get mine out of the broom closet."

"I already looked before I came down here, and it ain't there."

"Oh. Maybe I put it somewhere else after the last time we used it. Listen, let me finish up here and I'll meet you at the Sullivans' in about ten minutes."

"Sure. Okay." Pete continued to jockey for a peek inside and finally stood on tiptoe. "Is...uh...the puppy lady here?"

So that was it, Natalie thought. Maybe some of these folks would have been able to find a plunger elsewhere if this hadn't turned into such a good excuse to get a look at the crazy rich girl.

"She's here," Jonah said, resignation in his voice. "Would you like to meet her?"

"Oh, well, I didn't mean to foul up your evening. Leo said you two ran out on the setup at the Plaza."

"We did." Jonah stepped back. "Come on in, Pete," he said, turning toward Natalie. "Natalie LeBlanc, this is my neighbor Pete Hornacek."

"Glad to meet you." Natalie walked over to shake Pete's hand. He had blue eyes, white hair and a firm grip.

"Likewise." Pete's glance skimmed over the matching splotches on Natalie's dress and Jonah's shirt and his eyes twinkled. "Saw you two on the TV, sailing on that yacht. Nice boat."

"Wasn't it romantic?" Mrs. Sanchez said.

"Sure was," Pete said. "And how're you doin', *señora*? Leo says you been havin' your dizzy spells again."

Mrs. Sanchez smiled. "Got to expect that when you're almost ninety, Pete."

Natalie turned. "Almost ninety? Why, that's wonderful."

"It's God's will," Mrs. Sanchez said with a deep sigh. "Outlasted all my family. If I didn't have such good neighbors, I'd be in bad shape."

"The truth is, we weren't such good neighbors until this guy moved in," Pete said.

"Sure you were," Jonah said. "I—"

"He's right, *mihito*," Mrs. Sanchez interrupted. "We kept to ourselves."

Pete nodded. "Then along comes this big fireman from Buffalo who'd never met a stranger. Had a smile as wide as the Brooklyn Bridge and was ready to do anything for you. Why, one time—"

"Mrs. Sullivan must be wondering if she's ever going to get her sink unclogged." Jonah grabbed the dessert dishes. "How about if I rinse these and we get right on it, Pete?"

"I'll rinse the dishes." Natalie took them from him. "You get Mrs. Sanchez all tucked in for the night."

"Okay. Good idea." He smiled at her.

Pete was right about the charm of Jonah's smile, she thought. If she lived in this building, she'd feel extremely neighborly toward a man like Jonah.

"Oh, just leave the dishes," Mrs. Sanchez said with a wave of her hand. "You shouldn't be doing chores on your special night."

"It's my pleasure. I'm having a wonderful time." Which she was, she realized. Playing Tonto to Jonah's Lone Ranger was more satisfying than anything she'd done in a long time. Besides, eventually the neighbors would leave them alone, and the prospect of eventually having Jonah all to herself shimmered on the horizon, all the more tantalizing for being slightly out of reach.

Jonah leaned down and scooped Mrs. Sanchez into

his arms. "Come on, then, Scarlett O'Hara. Up the staircase with you."

Mrs. Sanchez giggled. "You're such a charmer, Rhett Butler."

"And you're such a beauty, Scarlett."

Natalie was bewitched by the sight of Jonah carrying the tiny woman into the bedroom. The image tugged at Natalie's heart, reminding her of when he'd cradled a cold and wet Bobo against his chest. If her mother could capture that tenderness on paper, she'd have a bestseller.

"He's quite a guy, isn't he?" Pete asked.

Natalie snapped out of her daze. "Uh, yes, he is. Well, I'd better get these rinsed." She started toward the kitchen.

"I'll keep you company." Pete followed her into the kitchen and leaned against the counter. "He hates it when I brag about him."

"I noticed." She turned on the kitchen faucet.

"But he just can't help doin' for others." He sent her a look that could be interpreted as a warning. "We think a lot of him around here."

"I can understand why."

"We wouldn't take kindly to anybody hurtin' him."

Natalie paused in the act of rinsing the bowls and looked at Pete. "I don't plan to hurt him." Shoot, if he refused to help her mother with the book, then she'd be the one on the short end of the stick. Of course, Pete had just said that Jonah was ready to help anybody with anything. That was encouraging.

"He musta decided the same thing if he brought you over here. Lately he's been real careful about lettin' people know where he lives."

"He told me that." Natalie stacked the dishes and

dried her hands on a towel threaded through the refrigerator handle. "I guess he's had some loony women after him."

"Begging your pardon, but that's what we figured you were, biddin' all that money just to go out with him."

"I can understand why you'd think that." She replaced the towel and turned to him. "But I'm not crazy."

Pete nodded. "I don't think so, either." He folded his arms. "So here's the way I have it figured. Your sweetheart was killed in the Persian Gulf, and it just so happened he looked like Jonah. So when Jonah shows up to save your puppy, you think maybe it's your sweetheart's spirit, coming to life in this other person, sort of like them time-travel stories. It's worth all that money to be with him and find out if he's your dead sweetheart come back to you. Am I right?"

Natalie grinned. "You're dead wrong. But it's a great concept." She couldn't help thinking that her mother would have a wonderful time talking to a man with Pete's imagination. Then an unfamiliar thought came to her. What if she introduced her mother to Pete? No, it was probably too soon. But, still…

"I'm wrong? Well, damn. Looks like I won't win the pool, then."

His strange comment chopped right into her thoughts. "Pool?"

"Everybody in the building who knows Jonah, and that's about all of them, wrote up their guess as to why you bid on him at the auction." He edged closer. "If you tell me, I won't tell anybody else. And I can't change my answer, because we put those in a sealed envelope and mailed it back to ourselves. It'll show up Monday."

"What'll show up Monday?" Jonah asked as he came into the kitchen.

Pete jumped. "Uh, Leo's plunger, most likely. That's when his daughter's supposed to bring it back. Is Mrs. Sanchez okay?" He looked nervous as he glanced at Natalie.

She returned his glance with a slight shake of her head. He obviously didn't want her to tell Jonah the whole apartment was betting on why this evening had taken place.

"She seems okay," Jonah said, eyeing both of them as if he suspected something was going on. "I checked her pulse and it's strong and steady. She's already asleep."

"Good." Pete frowned. "You don't s'pose she made that up about being dizzy just to get you over here, do you?"

Jonah's expression remained serious, but there was a sparkle in his dark eyes. "No more than you deliberately mislaid your plunger, Pete. Now let's go get mine."

8

ON THE WAY BACK to his apartment Jonah wondered how long his neighbors intended to play this little game. He would have been further ahead just to hold a reception for Natalie the minute they'd arrived in the building. But he couldn't be upset with them, no matter how frustrated he got. They weren't just curious, although that was part of it. Mostly they were trying to protect him by checking Natalie out.

They'd seen him make a mistake with Cynthia, and this woman from Central Park West seemed like an even bigger gamble. Funny how she'd managed to fit right in, though. As they approached his door she chatted away with Pete as if she'd known the guy forever.

They walked into the apartment where two glasses of warm, flat beer and an open can of peanuts sat on the coffee table. Jonah noticed a handful of peanuts dribbled on the floor next to the couch and remembered the moment Natalie had let them trickle out of her hand. The memory made it tough to draw a steady breath. He needed to find that damn plunger and send Pete on his way to the Sullivans'.

"So you checked the broom closet?" Jonah asked Pete.

"Sure did."

Jonah glanced at Natalie. "Excuse me a minute while I find the darn thing."

"Want me to help you look?" Her gray eyes teased him.

He gave her a tight-lipped smile. "Thanks. I'll handle it." He tore through the apartment in record time while Natalie and Pete continued their chummy conversation in the living room. He gathered they were talking about movies, and he was a little surprised to hear Pete's favorites were mostly sentimental stories. Natalie was bringing out a side of Pete that Jonah hadn't known existed.

Finally he found the plunger way in the back of his bedroom closet. Strange that it would be there, because he usually put things back more carefully than that. But he'd been pretty distracted lately, so anything was possible.

As he pulled the plunger out, it thumped against a small object on the floor of the closet. Then he remembered that's where he'd thrown the box of glow-in-the-dark condoms the guys at the station had given him. Just his luck they were the only ones he had, too.

Crouched in front of the closet, he stared at the box for a while and finally came to a decision. Only a fool would miss out on the chance to make love to Natalie because he was being choosy about condom style. Picking up the box, he opened it and put a condom in his pocket. Then he tossed the box into his bedside-table drawer before grabbing the plunger from the closet.

Before he left the bedroom, he glanced at the bed and pictured Natalie stretched out on it with the same teasing light in her eyes that had been there just a few minutes ago when she'd asked if he'd like some help looking for the plunger. His breath caught in his throat and his body tightened in anticipation. Once Pete was out the door...

"Hey, you found it," Pete said as Jonah walked into the room.

"Yep." Jonah handed it to him. "It's all yours."

Pete didn't reach to take the plunger. "Uh, Jonah, I—"

"Now what? Don't tell me. Beth's sink isn't really stopped up."

"Yeah, it's really stopped up. I don't even think she did it on purpose." He looked sheepish. "But I know she's hoping I'll show up with you and Natalie."

Jonah sighed.

"I promise she's the last one who wants to meet her," Pete said. "A lot of people are out tonight, it being Saturday and all. But Beth hasn't been talking about anything else for the past three days, and when she found out you and Natalie were in the building, she flipped. You know how it is, Jonah. She's stuck at home most of the time these days with them three babies, and your bachelor-auction date is like something out of a soap opera. Could you and Natalie come down for maybe a couple of minutes, just to say hello?"

Jonah was about to give in when he noticed the uneasy expression on Natalie's face. "It's up to you," he said.

"How old are these triplets?" Natalie asked, a definite hesitation in her voice.

"Four months," Jonah said. "They're probably asleep, anyway." Her reluctance surprised him after the way she'd been so eager to help the other people in the building. Maybe she didn't like babies. The minute that occurred to him, he discovered he wanted very much to know that about her. "I'm sure we won't even have to see them, if you'd don't want to."

"It's not that I don't want to see them. I...don't know anything about babies."

Pete chuckled. "I'll bet you could catch on quick. These little guys are real cute. I—"

"I don't think she's interested, Pete." Jonah's comment sounded harsher than he'd intended, and he realized with a shock that he was deeply disappointed in Natalie's reaction to seeing the triplets. She wasn't hesitating because she wanted to be alone with him instead, which would have suited him fine. She was hesitating because babies weren't her thing. That shouldn't mean squat to him, unless he'd begun spinning dreams about Natalie that he had no business spinning. The fact that he was crazy about kids and she wasn't meant nothing. Nothing at all.

Natalie sent him an assessing glance. "I think we should go."

"Look, you really don't have to. I'm sure you didn't pay good money so that you could—"

"I paid to be with you." Her gaze was steady. "So if you're going down to the Sullivans' apartment, so am I."

"You make it sound like you're heading off to an execution."

Pete glanced from one to the other. "She just said she wasn't used to babies, Jonah. That ain't no crime."

Jonah realized he was overreacting. It wasn't as if Natalie would ever be more than an interesting episode in his life. He really didn't care what she thought of babies. "You're right, Pete." He gave Natalie an apologetic smile. "Sorry."

"It's okay."

He could kick himself. She looked troubled, and he'd been a jerk to make such a big deal about nothing. "It's not okay, and I'll make it up to you. But first we need to get this out of the way. Let's go."

After the three of them filed out of his apartment, Jonah locked the door. Pete took the lead as they started down the hall and Jonah fell in beside Natalie.

"I get a little defensive about those triplets, I guess," Jonah said. "One of them is my godchild."

Pete glanced over his shoulder. "And Beth would sure appreciate it if you'd remember which one," he said with a chuckle.

"Hey, I can pick Matthew out."

"Two out of three tries. Half the time you think he's Michael or John."

"Are you saying you do better with yours? And Leo's hopeless. Last time he stood there saying eenie, meenie, minie, moe."

"Each of you is a godfather to one of the triplets?" Natalie asked.

"Yep," Pete said. "You shoulda seen the night they were born. Sully was workin', as usual, so Leo drove Beth to the hospital with me in the back seat, tryin' to keep her calm. Jonah begged for his chief's car to clear the way for Leo. With something like triplets, you don't want to take no chances."

"You sure don't." Jonah remembered he'd wanted to get an ambulance involved, but Beth had refused, so he'd done the next best thing and talked the chief out of his car.

"There are twins on my dad's side of the family," Natalie said. "My mother thinks I could have twins, but I just can't imagine it. And triplets...wow. It boggles my mind."

No doubt about it, Jonah thought. The woman wasn't yearning for motherhood anytime soon. That was good, in a way. If she'd been more open to the idea, he might have started thinking along really stupid lines. Just because he was physically attracted to her and she was cute and funny, he might have allowed himself to fall a little in love, which would lead naturally into imagining her as the mother of their children. At least that seemed to be the progression of his thoughts these days.

Until Beth's triplets had arrived, he hadn't considered kids, but that event seemed to have tripped a lever in his mind and now he thought about them a lot. He'd begun to envy his brother and two sisters because they all had families. A guy in that frame of mind could make a huge mistake if he let himself build dreams around the wrong woman. And for that kind of dream, Natalie was definitely the wrong woman.

As they neared the Sullivans' door, Jonah heard the unmistakable sound of Matthew, Michael and John all howling. Jonah had learned in the past four months that if one triplet started crying, the other two would soon follow. He glanced at Natalie. Her little frown of concern told him she wasn't looking forward to this.

"Sounds like the triplets aren't asleep, after all," she said.

"Want to go back up to the apartment and wait for me?" Jonah asked. "I'll be glad to give you the key."

"No." Her chin lifted. "I'll stay."

Jonah smiled at the resolution in her expression. She was so damn pretty in her red dress that he'd be content to stand there looking at her forever. He wanted to reach out and brush his thumb over her smooth cheek, but now wasn't the time for such things.

"Those babies will settle down once they see their uncle Pete and uncle Jonah." Pete pushed the doorbell, leaving his finger on the button so the sound would carry over the babies' wailing.

Beth flung open the door. Her long curly hair was haphazardly caught back with a butterfly clip and she held a red-faced, screaming baby. "Thank God," she said, thrusting the baby at Pete. "Hold Michael while I get John and Matthew out of their cribs. The neighbors must be going crazy." She hurried out of the room.

"Is the clog in the kitchen?" Jonah called after her.

"Yeah! Have at it!" she called back.

Jonah headed for the kitchen where water stood three inches deep in the sink. He pushed up his sleeves and went to work with the plunger as the sound of crying babies continued. He felt sorry for Beth, who was very conscious of disturbing the young couple who had just moved into the apartment right above hers.

He also doubted she'd envisioned a scene like this when she talked Pete into bringing him down here with Natalie. At the time, the kids had probably been sound asleep and she was so eager to get a glimpse of his date for the night that she'd told herself the triplets would stay asleep until her longed-for company had left.

The clog was a stubborn one. He'd finally loosened it when he became aware that the babies weren't crying anymore. He heard footsteps and turned as Beth came into the kitchen with Matthew. At least he thought it was Matthew. Could have been John. Each of the babies had the same curly dark hair, the same blue eyes, the same cute baby stare.

"Looks like you got it loose," Beth said. "Thanks, Jonah."

"No problem." Yep, he was pretty sure she was holding Matthew, who had a cowlick the other two didn't. That left John unaccounted for. "Did you put John back to bed?"

Beth chuckled. "This is John."

"Curses, foiled again." He turned back to the sink and gave the drain a couple of extra pumps. "So where's Matthew?"

"Natalie has him. You know, she's not anything like I thought she'd be."

He swiveled back to her so abruptly he almost hit his nose on the plunger handle. "*Natalie* has Matthew?"

"Why are you so surprised?"

"She seemed sort of worried about coming in contact with triplets."

Beth laughed. "Everybody is worried about coming in contact with triplets. They're intimidating. They—pull your hair! Hey, kid, let go." She paused to loosen John's grip on a lock of her hair. "I can tell she hasn't been around babies much, but once I plopped Matthew in her lap she did fine."

"No kidding?"

Beth gazed at him. "No kidding. I like her, Jonah. She can't help it if she's rich, you know. And she did just give a chunk of it away at the bachelor auction, so she's not as rich as she was a week ago."

Jonah grimaced. "I have a feeling it was a drop in the bucket." He shook water off the plunger and tore off a paper towel from a roll by the sink. "I like her, too." That was a whopper of an understatement, he thought, considering how desperately he wanted her. "But I have a hard time getting around that whole business of the auction. How can I possibly have something in common with a woman who would throw around that kind of money?"

Beth transferred John to her other hip. "Don't forget, it wasn't just to spend the weekend with you. The proceeds went to literacy, and I know you support that. There's something you have in common—helping everyone learn to read."

They had much more in common than an interest in literacy, Jonah thought. When Natalie was in his arms, they seemed to be created for each other, at least physically. "I keep thinking this is just a one-time thrill for her," he said.

"Maybe, but from the short time I've been around her, I don't see her that way. I say give her a chance. Don't be prejudiced against her just because she has money."

Jonah grinned at her as he finished drying off the plunger. "Seems to me only yesterday you warned me about getting too involved with some crazy rich woman."

Beth smiled back at him. "That was before she started cooing over Matthew."

"Uh-huh." *This* Jonah had to see. In the meantime, John was straining toward Jonah and holding out his little arms. Jonah held the plunger toward Beth. "Here. I'll trade you."

"Gladly. These guys are getting to be heavyweights."

"That's their job." Jonah gathered the little boy into his arms with a sigh of contentment. "Hey, John. How's the world treating you, tiger?"

John patted Jonah's cheeks and made little gurgling sounds as he bounced in Jonah's arms.

"That good, huh? Give me five." He tapped his hand against the baby's palm. "Atta boy."

"Jonah, how much longer are you going to deprive yourself of kids?" Beth said. "Guys with no talent for being a father are reproducing like crazy, and here you are still single and childless."

"Blame Natalie." Jonah tickled John under the chin and the baby laughed.

"Natalie?"

"If she hadn't lost her dog in the lake, I'd be seriously dating some wonderful woman by now. Instead, I've been forced into hiding. I don't dare even smile at a girl on the subway, let alone ask somebody out."

"You have a date tonight."

"Yeah, with the woman who caused all the trouble, a woman who can buy and sell me. Come to think of it, that's exactly what she did."

Beth leaned toward him and brushed her hand over his shoulder.

"What? Am I shedding?"

She gazed at him. "No, I was just trying to get that big chip off."

Jonah rolled his eyes at her.

"Now, come on in the living room and see how sweet she looks holding Matthew."

"Yes, ma'am." As he followed Beth through the small dining area and into the living room, he wondered if she might be right about his attitude. Natalie didn't ask to be rich, and to her credit she'd donated a chunk of her money to a worthy cause. Maybe she wasn't crazy at all, and she'd needed the tax deduction. Maybe she'd thought a special weekend would be a nice chance to thank him for saving her dog.

That left the mystery of her special request unsolved,

but that might have something to do with charity, too. She could be associated with some nonprofit group that planned a fund-raiser and she wanted him to be part of it. The idea of more time spent in the public eye made him wince, but if she asked, he might consider it.

As he neared the living room, he heard laughter and happy little baby sounds, but he wasn't prepared for the sight that greeted him. Natalie sat on the couch with Matthew in her lap. She'd turned so that her knees almost touched Pete's, who was holding Michael. With the help of the two adults, the kids were playing patty-cake. It required complete concentration on everybody's part, and they all seemed oblivious to anything outside their little circle.

Beth paused in the doorway, and he stood beside her, fascinated by the sight of Natalie playing with the two babies. He'd always been a sucker for a woman with a child, but watching Natalie with Matthew was like seeing the pieces of his world click firmly into place. She was a natural—someday she'd have her own babies and play with them exactly the same way.

She'd said there were twins in her family. Jonah had no trouble imagining the scene with two girls, both towheads, and Jonah's father sitting there instead of Pete. He felt a tug of desire combined with a possessive urge so strong it took his breath away.

"See what I mean?" Beth murmured.

Jonah swallowed. "Yeah."

Pete and Natalie sang out the final words of the nursery rhyme. *And put it in the oven for baby and me.*

As Natalie patted Matthew's hands together while he squealed in delight, she glanced up, a happy smile on her face.

Jonah wanted to bottle that smile. He met her gaze

and a zing of wild emotion arrowed straight to his so-
lar plexus.

"Did you fix the sink?" she asked.

"Yep, all fixed. You seem to have made a couple of
friends."

"We've had a good time," she said, sounding surprised about it.

"I can tell." He knew he was staring at her like an idiot, but he was completely absorbed by the picture she
made with a chortling baby in her lap. All sorts of images flashed through his mind—what she'd look like
round and pregnant, the joy on her face as she held her
newborn, the tenderness with which she'd bring the
small mouth to her breast.

"You know what, Beth," Pete said. "I think we've
taken up enough of these folks' time. How about lettin'
them go home and I'll help you put the Three Stooges
to bed."

"Fine by me," Beth said.

Jonah snapped out of his trance. He was imagining
Natalie giving birth to their child and he hadn't even
made love to her yet. But that was about to change. "If
you're sure everything's okay here," he said, trying not
to sound too eager. He hadn't been this excited about
being alone with a woman since the days of back-seat
makeout sessions.

"We're fine," Beth said. "I appreciate you two coming by."

"I'm glad we did," Natalie said. "Your babies are
beautiful."

"I'm glad we did, too," Jonah said as he handed John
over to Beth.

She winked at him. "Nice clean shoulder you have
there."

"Thanks."

After giving each of the babies several more kisses, Jonah and Natalie left the Sullivans' apartment.

"What was that about a clean shoulder?" Natalie asked once the door closed behind them.

"I'll explain later." Heart thudding in anticipation, Jonah took her hand in his and started down the hall. The time for talking was over.

9

BABIES.

Natalie hadn't given them much thought. Most of the women she knew married later and delayed motherhood until they had a good handle on their careers. At twenty-eight she'd always thought she had tons of time to worry about babies.

But that was before she'd seen Jonah standing in the doorway with a four-month-old cherub in his arms.

She'd never forget the image. With his shirtsleeves pushed back and his hair rumpled, he looked so much like a daddy that it brought a lump to her throat. But this was no ordinary daddy. His broad shoulders and powerful physique dwarfed the tiny boy he cradled against his chest. The contrast between heroic man and vulnerable child was so tender she couldn't tear her gaze away. When John reached up and patted Jonah's cheek, she melted.

She'd stayed in that liquified state as they said their goodbyes and headed down the hall and up the stairs toward Jonah's apartment. Her bones felt rubbery and her blood hot. She wasn't in the best condition in which to explain her mother's project, but she was helpless to change things. Jonah's grasp on her hand was firm, and the connection kept heat flowing between them. She was simmering, and it would only take a gentle touch in just the right place to make her boil right over.

That touch came after Jonah led her inside and locked the door. Without speaking, he slid his hand to the nape of her neck. When Bobo was smaller, she'd been able to pick him up that way and he'd immediately gone limp as a noodle. As Jonah massaged her skin and gazed deep into her eyes, she had no more resistance than a puppy.

A hint of a smile curved his mouth and crinkled the corners of his eyes.

"Yes," she whispered.

The flame flickering in his eyes grew brighter. "Just like that?"

"Just like that." She was quivering so much she could barely stand.

In a heartbeat she was scooped into the same strong arms that had saved her dog, carried Mrs. Sanchez and cradled a small baby. It was, she decided, a very special place to be.

Jonah continued to hold her gaze as he carried her through the bedroom door and laid her gently on the bed. Still watching her as if she might vanish in a puff of smoke, he began unbuttoning his shirt.

Her heart thudded with excitement as he took off the shirt, his chest muscles flexing with the motion.

"I'm no different from any other guy you know." He nudged off his shoes and pulled off his socks before reaching for the buckle of his belt.

She quivered. "I doubt it." A man built like a Greek statue with the heart of a saint didn't come along every day.

"I have three overdue library books and I squeeze the toothpaste tube in the middle." He unbuckled the belt and pulled it from the loops in one smooth motion. "I never miss a Knicks game on TV and I'll put ketchup on just about anything but ice cream."

"Sounds fun." Her voice was thick and sultry, almost unrecognizable to her. She'd never been so hungry for a man in her life.

He paused in the act of unfastening his pants, and his eyebrows lifted.

She moistened her dry lips. "I've never tried it with ketchup."

There it was, that look he'd given her when he'd caught her wiping strawberry juice from her blouse. His hands trembled as he unzipped his pants and stepped out of them. His voice was strained. "Do you want me to go get the bottle?"

"No," she whispered. Gazing at his arousal straining against the cotton of his briefs, she knew this was a moment that needed no embellishment. She looked into his eyes. "All I need is you."

He put one knee on the bed and leaned over her. "I wonder if that will be enough."

She smiled, thinking of the sizable bulge of his manhood. She reached up and cradled his face in both hands. "Oh, I think you will be more than enough." With a sigh she drew him down.

IF HE HADN'T WANTED HER more than he wanted to take his next breath, Jonah might have been worried about making love to a woman who thought ketchup would make an interesting sex toy. He tried to keep his brain functioning, tried to keep from losing himself in the experience. But with the first touch of her velvet lips, he felt as if he'd dived into a vat of warm honey.

Everything faded from his consciousness—the ever-present traffic outside the window, the slam of a door in the next apartment, the bark of a dog. The world constricted to the width and length of this bed and the presence of this woman. He was engulfed by the sound of her breathing, the scent of her skin, the texture of her hair.

Her kiss—open, moist, ready—was flavored with new meaning. She had said yes—yes to him, his touch, and his ultimate invasion. The promise of that heated his body like nothing had done before. Control disappeared as need drove him relentlessly. He understood the instinct for survival, had believed that was all that remained of a primitive genetic code.

He'd been wrong.

For the first time in his life, he bowed to the unmistakable instinct to mate. Like a salmon swimming upstream, he forged his way along a river of sensation, intent on joining with this woman. His heart, against all reason, had chosen her, and now his heart would not be denied. He fought the barrier of her clothes, and what refused to give way was wrenched and torn, sometimes with her own hands. Her mangled dress landed in a heap on the floor, closely followed by her underwear. They were both panting in anticipation as he removed the last scrap of material and encountered nothing but a glorious expanse of warm skin.

He laid his hand over her pounding heart, imprinting himself there. She would never forget this joining, he vowed, and neither would he. Deepening his kiss, he drank her moan of satisfaction as he skimmed his hand over every inch of her he could reach.

Now. Now he would begin the sweet journey. Round, firm breasts, silken thighs, a welcoming channel drenched with passion—he explored them all, revisited them all as she twisted and cried out beneath his caress.

With the taste of her on his tongue, the scent of her filling his nostrils, the feel of her humming through his fingertips, he returned to look deep into those soft gray eyes. They sought his gaze with a fevered desperation. Her pupils were wide with desire, her cheeks flushed with passion.

"Please," she whispered through kiss-swollen lips.

He pulled off his briefs and forced himself to take a condom from the bedside-table drawer. Putting it on was his last rational act before he eased between her warm thighs. She grasped his hips and arched upward in the most eloquent invitation he'd ever received. Arms braced on either side of her head, he watched her face as he sank slowly, smoothly into her heat. Her eyes widened and her breath came in tiny gasps from between her parted lips.

Then the gasps took shape, and he realized she was saying his name in breathless little puffs of sound. It was a chant of total vulnerability, of complete surrender, of absolute trust. His chest tightened with joy.

At last he was buried deep within her. "I'm here," he murmured.

"Yes." Her eyes glowed with fulfillment.

He leaned down and brushed her mouth with his. The tension coiled between them made that butterfly kiss flash like a rocket across his senses. He could be still no longer.

"Move with me," he said, drawing back and thrusting forward. "Dance with me, Natalie."

Her hips rose to meet his as she caught his rhythm, matching him thrust for thrust. He groaned with pleasure as each contact rippled through him, bringing his trembling body closer and closer to the edge. He sensed the quickening deep within her and watched with fierce satisfaction as a flush spread over her damp skin, tinging her the color of morning, the color of beginnings.

Her gaze held his. He reveled in the climax building in the depths of her eyes, rejoiced that she didn't close them and deprive him of his reward. He learned the movement that stoked the fire. There. And again. And again. She whimpered. Once more. Yes.

With a wild cry she arched upward, and that graceful arch proved his own undoing. He exploded into pure energy. As wave after wave of ecstasy crashed over him, he looked into her luminous eyes and held himself deep inside her, letting her feel the intensity, the outpouring. Yet under all the glory ran a thread of disappointment. Despite the power and the mind-numbing delight, the rush of completion had smashed against a barrier. The mating, the soul-to-soul joining that he had pursued with such desperation was, in the end, incomplete.

But they had begun. He could see it in her eyes. They had really, truly begun.

NATALIE LAY LOOKING UP into the incredible beauty of Jonah's face and knew she was no longer the same woman who had been carried into this bedroom. The depth of his lovemaking had changed her, creating new horizons, exotic dreams.

"Be right back," he whispered. In moments he'd returned and gathered her into his arms. He combed damp strands of hair from her forehead. "And what was it," he began, his voice still husky in the aftermath of passion, "that you wanted to ask me?"

So bathed in sensuality that she could scarcely think, it took her a minute to understand him. Oh, yes. Her mother's book. "Not now," she murmured, unwilling to risk spoiling the wondrous experience they'd just shared.

His smile was slow and lazy. "Most women would think now was a perfect time. I probably couldn't say no to anything you wanted."

She stroked his back, loving the sculpted contours of muscle and sinew. "I'm not most women."

"I'm figuring that out." He nuzzled the base of her throat and took a deep breath. "Mmm. Sweet. Like the flowers I used to pick in the woods and bring to my mother."

She should have known he'd been that sort of little boy. She arched her neck, loving the way he nibbled and licked his way up to her chin. "I'm glad you like it," she murmured.

"I do." He nipped gently at her earlobe. "I just wish I could afford to buy it for you."

A slight chill moved over her. She really hated having him think she was filthy rich when she wasn't. "It's not very expensive cologne."

He began to chuckle, his breath soft against her skin. "God, Natalie, I destroyed your dress. Your beautiful dress. Here I'm worried about buying you cologne and I've probably ruined some designer outfit worth hundreds of dollars. Damn. I've never ripped a woman's clothes off in my life. You'd think I could have picked an outfit from a bargain basement."

"You did."

He lifted his head and gazed down at her. "You bought a bargain-basement dress to go to the Plaza?"

"Sure. Why not?"

He smiled and shook his head. "I just didn't think—well, never mind. Beth accused me of having an attitude about your money and I guess she's right. That's what she was talking about when we were leaving her apartment. She thought I'd finally shrugged the chip off my shoulder."

So he was beginning to accept the fact she was wealthy. She wondered what would happen if later on he found out she wasn't wealthy, that she'd let him believe it because she couldn't admit to spending her retirement money without feeling like a fool.

She hadn't thought any of that would matter, but then, she hadn't thought she'd be lying next to a very naked and very sexy Jonah, either.

"The dress wasn't expensive, but even if it had been, I wouldn't have cared," she admitted. "You see, nobody's ever ripped my clothes off, either. I didn't know it could be so much…fun."

His gaze smoldered. "Don't get me wrong. I'm not apologizing." He leaned down and kissed her slowly and thoroughly before reaching down and pulling up a quilt that was folded across the end of the bed. As he tucked it around her, he feathered a kiss against her cheek. "Stay warm. I'll be back in no time."

He hadn't been gone more than two seconds before her conscience began to prick her. If only she'd already told him about her mother's project, then she could relax and fully enjoy this incredible experience. But she couldn't shake the notion that he wasn't the sort of man who appreciated a woman keeping secrets from him. And she was keeping more than one.

She would tell him now, she decided, before things progressed any further between them. Leaving the bed, she wrapped the quilt around her and went in search of her hero. It was hard to concentrate on business while she was feeling so loose and well loved, but she had to do it.

She tracked him to the kitchen, where he was getting them each a fresh beer. As she padded barefoot into the kitchen, trailing a part of the quilt like a train, her entrance was so quiet he obviously didn't hear her. For a brief moment she stood looking at him, gloriously naked, pouring the first beer into a tall glass. A quiver of need spiraled through her and settled deep in the spot he'd so recently awakened. The ache of longing began once again.

He glanced up and smiled as he continued to pour. "The dress was dynamite, but you look pretty good in that quilt, too." He finished the first bottle and twisted the cap off the second.

Natalie tried not to be distracted from her mission. She had to start talking, and fast. But when he twisted off the bottle cap, his muscles flexed in a most inviting way. Her little speech about her mother hovered on her lips. But it seemed so inappropriate, considering how delicious Jonah looked at the moment.

"I happen to like your outfit, too," she said. She'd been so busy enjoying his inspired touch that she hadn't taken the time to touch him in return. She wanted to do that. She wanted to do that now.

She let the quilt slide to the floor.

Apparently the swish it made when it landed caught his attention, because he looked in her direction…and promptly poured beer on the counter. Grabbing a dishrag, he started to mop up the spill.

"Wait." A living god like Jonah could put all sorts of sensuous ideas in a girl's head. "Don't waste it." She walked over to the counter and leaned down to lick up a bit of liquid and foam. Then she glanced up at him and ran her tongue around her lips.

A fire ignited in the depths of his eyes.

Spurred to even greater lengths, she leaned down again and swirled her tongue over the small puddle of beer. This time when she looked up he'd become rigid as a statue, including the part of him that she had designs on. She reached out and encircled him with her fingers, loving the contrast of silky skin sheathing his powerful erection. The sight and feel of his body brought out a primitive yearning in her that she was helpless to deny.

His breathing became uneven as the fire raged in his eyes. With deliberate intent she went to her knees.

He drew in a quick breath, but he didn't stop her. The knowledge that he wanted this as much as she did surged through her veins like hot lava. The blood roared in her ears, muting his soft moan as she took him into her mouth.

And how she loved him—delighting in every gasp, every groan, every quiver of his sculpted body. For the first time in her life she longed to give pleasure to a man even more than she wanted to take her own. And there was no doubt it was pleasure she was giving. He whispered her name, his voice rich with tension, as a fine trembling took him.

Her heart swelled as she realized how vulnerable he was at this moment, when she was about to strip him of all control. Then firmly and tenderly, she did exactly that. His guttural cry rained down on her as she took all he had to give.

Only when he lifted her to her feet and kissed her fervently did she register the deep, pounding desire in herself. Before she quite realized how he'd done it, he'd urged her back to the floor, back onto the quilt she'd dropped. His mouth found all the burning, aching places on her passion-flushed body, and at last he slipped his hands beneath her hips and lavished attention on her as she had on him, returning tenfold the gift she'd given.

After the glory of it splashed over her and receded a little, leaving her more content than anyone had a right to be, she lay cocooned with Jonah in the quilt. She put her head on his chest and listened to his steady heartbeat. Jonah's heart. He stroked her hair and kissed the top of her head. Jonah's hand. Jonah's lips.

She was with Jonah. With a sharpness that was almost painful, she realized how much she wanted to be with him long after this weekend was over. Her scheme, still hidden from him, loomed larger every moment. He would understand, she told herself. He would be happy to help. But the thing was, she didn't really know. And she was very afraid to find out.

As NATALIE'S HOST, Jonah decided he should offer her the chance to sleep. Tomorrow could be a challenging day as they both tried to return to their normal routine with the media hot on their tails. He didn't have the heart to point it out yet, but after tonight's escape from the Plaza she'd probably have as many reporters hounding her as he did. She wouldn't like the attention, and she'd need some rest in order to deal with it.

So he put on his briefs and even suggested she unpack whatever nightgown she'd brought to wear in her suite at the Plaza. But when she pulled out a frothy pink number and held it up, he shook his head.

"You don't like it?" she asked.

"I like it a lot. If you put that on, we won't sleep."

"What's your point?" Her smile of invitation made his pulse rate climb.

"I'm afraid I'm going to wear you out." He couldn't believe it, but he wanted her again, less than a half hour after the kitchen episode. He wondered if he'd be able to fix a meal in there ever again without getting hard. Even the beer, which usually had a calming effect on his libido, hadn't put a dent in his craving for her.

"Why don't you let me decide if I'm worn-out or not?"

He shook his head. "I'm determined to let you sleep, at least for a little while. Let's see what I can come up with." He crossed to his dresser and dug through the bottom drawer. Finally he found an old FDNY T-shirt. After many washings it was frayed and faded to sidewalk-gray. It shouldn't look sexy on anyone. As long as she wore the T-shirt, he told himself, he'd be able to leave her alone for a couple of hours, which would make him feel more like a civilized man and less like a ravenous beast.

He hadn't counted on the hole. When she pulled it over her head it reached to midthigh, and she looked like a little kid in her big brother's shirt—until she moved and one pert nipple poked out of the hole over her right breast.

She glanced down, then looked up at him, mischief in her eyes. "Peekaboo."

He groaned. "Put it on backward."

"But I like it this way." She slipped her finger in the hole. "I'll bet this would tear away in no time."

He struggled for self-control and found enough to reach over and flip off the wall switch, plunging the room into darkness. "We're going to bed to sleep," he said firmly.

"If you say so. Which side do you want?"

Gradually his eyes grew adjusted to the darkness and he could see her standing at the end of the bed. He didn't have a particular side because he'd never shared a bed with anyone long enough to establish a pattern. Yet he answered from instinct. "The side closest to the door." Without even thinking, he'd put himself between her and any potential danger. In the space of a few hours she'd become so precious to him that he wanted to protect her from all harm.

She walked to the far side of the bed and climbed in.

As he watched her slide under the covers, a wave of tenderness swept over him, and he stood there wondering why that small action should stir him so. Finally it occurred to him that this little scene of a man and woman quietly climbing into the same bed, supposedly to sleep, was quite domestic. The thought of sharing the same bed with Natalie night after night held more than sexual appeal. Until now, he hadn't understood the depth of his longing for a wife, for children, for a home. Sex wasn't the only thing he wanted from this woman.

Yeah, right. The minute he climbed into the bed, he felt her heat calling to him. She snuggled close and her exposed nipple brushed his arm. He could tell by the firmness of it that she was aroused.

"Good night," she whispered.

"Good night." He lay there fighting his imagination. There *would* have to be a hole in the T-shirt. Right where he could lean down and taste her. And she'd deliberately stuck her finger in the hole to remind him of how much fun it would be to widen the hole, to tear that old T-shirt right away and—"Oh, hell."

She was giggling from the moment he grabbed her.

How he loved turning those giggles into gasps of pleasure. The T-shirt gave way with a satisfying rip, and he
feasted on her breasts until they were both wild and
straining toward the moment of connection. He fumbled in the drawer and took out a condom.

Breathing hard, she grabbed it away from him. "Let
me."

"Be quick."

"I will."

He squeezed his eyes shut and clenched his jaw so
that he'd last through the sensation of Natalie unroll-
ing the condom over his throbbing erection.

"Oh!"

At her startled cry, he opened his eyes and looked at
her, but he couldn't see her expression in the dark. He
could, however, see his penis. It was glowing.

"I'll be damned."

Her voice was choked with suppressed laughter.
"You didn't know?"

"The guys at the station…"

"For tonight?" She giggled.

"For tonight."

Her laughter filled the room. "You look like…" She
paused and gulped back fresh giggles. "You look like
you just sprouted your own personal Jedi light saber!"

It was pretty damn funny, but he had other things on
his mind. "I did," he said, rolling her to her back. "And
you're about to feel the power of the Force."

She continued to laugh as she wound her arms
around his neck. "Will you make me light up, too?"

"Guaranteed, Princess." He pushed deep inside her.
Home.

10

SOMETIME DURING THE NIGHT, as he slept a little and made love to Natalie a lot, Jonah admitted to himself he'd been wrong to judge her by her wealth. His initial reaction when he'd first seen her playing in the park with Bobo was the one that counted. Her outrageous bidding at the bachelor auction had thrown him off track, making him think she was a flake.

Instead, she was everything he dreamed of in a woman.

By the time they sat across the breakfast table from each other sipping coffee and smiling whenever their glances met, he'd decided he was in love. That would explain his goofy delight in hearing Sunday church bells, someone whistling on the street below and the sound of a child running down the hall.

Breakfast wasn't much to brag about. He'd managed to scare up some bread for toast and a jar of grape jelly, plus the coffee. But she hadn't seemed to care, and he certainly wasn't concerned about food. The only problem they had, as near as he could tell, was that the media would descend on them the minute they appeared in public. He'd already begun plotting ways they could escape and spend the day alone together. He wanted to wander with her among wildflowers and green grass, perky songbirds and sunshine. Yep, he had it bad.

He reached across the table and laced his fingers

through hers. "Your dog cost you a lot of money, you know."

"Bobo?" She rubbed her thumb against his palm. "Why do you say that?"

Even such a simple caress made him want her. He couldn't get over the effect she had on him. She wore one of his Knicks T-shirts this morning because the FDNY one had been reduced to rags. This one had no holes in it, unfortunately, so he'd probably just do the normal thing and pull it over her head.

But he ought to at least let her finish her toast, so he continued the conversation and let his anticipation build for what would happen after breakfast. "Well, it's just that we didn't need that stunt of Bobo's to bring us together," he said. "I would have asked you out eventually, anyway."

"Really?" She looked totally surprised.

"Sure. I'd seen you at the park several times, and there was never a guy with you, so I was hoping you were single. I'd planned to stop and talk to you soon."

"Is that right?" The concept seemed to completely capture her attention. "I had no idea."

"Which means you didn't notice me on my afternoon runs." He grinned at her. "I guess I should be insulted."

"I'm sorry to say I didn't notice you. I can't imagine why, but everything worked out for the best, anyway."

"I'm sure the literacy people feel that way. But frankly, I wish we'd met in a normal way and you'd just quietly donated to the cause and taken your tax deduction. It's been a rough few months for me."

She squeezed his hand. "I'm sorry about that."

"Water over the dam." He looked into her gray eyes. Damn, but he was happy. "Right this minute I'm not nearly as sorry as I used to be. In fact, I'd go through it all again if I knew you'd be waiting for me at the end of the line."

Her expression softened. "That's a very sweet thing to say."

"You've made the torture worthwhile." There was more, much more, he could admit, but he hesitated. She seemed to be as involved as he was, but this was a delicate part in any relationship. They'd shared a fantastic night, and he thought they were building a foundation for more fantastic nights, but he wasn't completely sure if she would agree. "I guess you must have felt something click between us when I saved your dog," he said, fishing a little.

"Well, I—"

"I mean, it's pretty hard for me to believe that you'd spend that money just to thank me. You had to be thinking there might be something between us to go that high in the bidding." He waited for her ready agreement, and when it didn't come, his heartbeat kicked up a notch. The longer he waited, the faster his heart pounded. He wasn't happy with the uncertain look in her eyes.

Oh, God, maybe she was trying to decide how to let him down easy. Maybe all she'd wanted was a one-night stand with the local hero, and she had no intention of linking up permanently with a guy who didn't match her financial status. The coffee and toast began to roll in his stomach.

She took a breath. "Actually, I—"

"Hey." His head throbbed and his gut churned with acute disappointment. He'd just made a fool of himself. He shoved back his chair and stood. "Forget I said anything. Obviously I'm way off base here. I thought—

well, never mind what I thought." He was desperate to end the moment. "Listen, feel free to use the shower and get cleaned up if you want. I'll call you a cab. You're probably eager to be on your way, and I've been keeping you."

"Jonah! Please sit down. There's something I need to tell you, something I should have told you before, but we were having such a wonderful time and I hated to—"

"You're married to an old geezer in a rest home."

"No. If you'll just—"

"You're married to some international tycoon you hardly ever see."

"No! I'm not married at all! Please sit down."

So she wasn't married. He didn't have to face that particular nightmare. But he couldn't sit down. The way his insides were heaving around, he might have to excuse himself to go into the bathroom and be sick to his stomach. "Just say it, Natalie. I should have known this was too good to be true, that you were too good to be true."

"I wish you wouldn't jump to conclusions like this." She stood, apparently needing the movement as much as he did. "Okay, here's what happened." Her voice trembled slightly, and she began to pace, tapping her clasped hands against her chin.

He took some satisfaction in her nervousness. At least it wasn't easy for her to explain to him that he'd been had, literally.

"My mother saw the news the night you rescued Bobo."

"Didn't everybody."

"You inspired her to start writing a romance novel with…with you as the hero. She tried to get in touch

with you to get more information, but you were unreachable, so when I saw that you'd be in the bachelor
auction, I..." She glanced at him. "Oh, Jonah, don't
look like that."

He wondered how the hell she expected him to look.
The idea of some society matron amusing herself by
writing a romance using him as one of the main characters gave him a case of hives. But there was a deeper
issue here.

He'd gone into this weekend like an eager pup, tail
wagging, thinking that Natalie hadn't been able to re-
sist his charms, when all she'd really wanted was some
information for her mother's book. No wonder she'd
been so delighted to see his apartment. No wonder
she'd asked about his firefighting injuries. No wonder
she'd been so interested in his family background. *And
no wonder she'd wanted to make love to him.* The thought
that their night's activities could show up in her
mother's manuscript made him want to hit something.

He cleared his throat. "So is that what last night was
about?" he asked quietly. "Research?"

"No!"

He turned away, unable to accept her denial in the
face of all the damning evidence to the contrary. He'd
always wondered how laboratory animals felt, forced
against their will to be part of some godlike creature's
experiment. Right now he had a pretty good idea, and
his reaction was unprintable. "I wish I could believe
you, but after all, you spent thirty-three thousand dollars to help your mother get information about me.
Even for someone as well off as you, that's not exactly
chump change. It's only logical that you'd want to get
your money's worth."

She gasped as if she'd been slapped.

He glanced back at her.

Her face had lost all color and she had a death grip on the back of the kitchen chair. "Is that what you really think?"

"Let's put it this way. Your mother gets the notion to write a romance, and you casually pay out thousands to rope me into helping out. I can't relate to that kind of behavior, Natalie, so I couldn't begin to guess how you operate. I figure anything's possible."

"Just like that, you'd judge me guilty."

He tried to get past the ache in his heart and find out if he was being too hasty. But when he added up the facts, he still came to the same conclusion. Natalie had said her mother "understood" the outlay of money, so apparently they'd plotted together to buy his cooperation, using Natalie as the bait. It was a game they were playing, and they had the money to play it.

"You don't have to answer," she murmured. "I can see it in your eyes. Give me five minutes to get dressed and I'll be out of here."

Although he knew that was the only possible outcome, he still fought a sense of panic, knowing she was about to walk out of his life forever. "You don't have to—"

"If you have no more respect for me than that, I do. And don't bother about a cab. I'll walk to the corner and find one. I wouldn't want you to compromise your security." She walked past him and down the hall to the bedroom, closing the door quietly behind her.

Jonah rubbed a hand over his face. Was he making a terrible mistake? If she'd frantically begged him to change his mind, if she'd even resorted to tears, he might have been more sure of his judgment, more sure she was simply continuing to manipulate him for the sake of her mother's book. But her icy calm and her dignified exit made him doubt himself.

She acted as if she thought her behavior was perfectly justified, though God knows how she could rationalize it that way. Perhaps she'd admit she should have told him sooner, but other than that, she apparently didn't see a thing wrong with her actions. She didn't think this plan to buy him and use him for her mother's new hobby demeaned either him or his profession. But he felt demeaned. And most of all he was deeply hurt that she hadn't wanted him for himself.

Did she really expect him to play lapdog for the rich ladies and be a role model for a romance-novel hero? He shuddered at the thought. It would be worse than parading naked down Fifth Avenue. Besides, there was the danger that Natalie's mother would get the damn thing published. With her financial resources she could probably pay to have it published herself. Then she could very well decide to use his local fame as a springboard for sales. What a disaster that would be.

Natalie appeared in the kitchen doorway dressed in her white sweatshirt and slacks, her small suitcase in one hand, her purse over her shoulder. "Thanks for a wonderful weekend." Her eyes glistened.

His stomach clutched as he realized she was about to cry. No matter how shallow her original motives might have been, they'd shared something special during the night, and she obviously didn't like this parting any more than he did.

"Natalie, can't you see that I—"

"I can see that I shouldn't have tried this in the first place." Her voice was shaky but resolute. "It was pretty stupid of me. Goodbye, Jonah.'' She turned and walked toward the front door.

He wanted to stop her from leaving, but he didn't know what he could say that would make everything okay. A short while ago he'd kidded himself that they lived in the same world, after all. Now he understood that they were light-years apart.

BLINDED BY HER TEARS, furious with Jonah and even more furious with herself, Natalie decided to keep walking until she got a grip on her emotions. With her sunglasses firmly in place, nobody would be able to tell she was crying, and the brisk movement helped. She'd find a cab when she'd calmed down. *If* she calmed down. The way she felt at the moment, she might have to hoof it the length of Manhattan.

Damn Jonah. How could he possibly think the only reason she'd made love to him was to get material for her mother's book? She'd bared her soul to him, letting him know her in ways that no one else on this earth did, and yet this morning he was ready to believe the worst about her.

Well, to hell with him. If he was that quick to condemn her, he was no hero, either for her or her mother's book. A small voice suggested that maybe she'd handled the evening poorly, that she should have found a way to tell him about the book before they made love. But that still didn't excuse Jonah's rush to judgment. He'd seen into her very heart, and he should have been willing to give her the benefit of the doubt. He should have been willing to at least talk about her mother's project.

She'd considered telling him about Alice's depression and why writing this book was so important, but his attitude had been so hostile that she was damned if she'd reveal more personal information about her family and her problems. Maybe he didn't believe rich people got depressed. Beth Sullivan was right about his attitude toward wealth—he had a massive chip on his shoulder. Because he assumed her mother was rich, he also assumed her book was a silly little hobby that meant nothing.

The more she thought about his prejudiced reaction, the angrier she got, until she was practically race-walking down the sidewalk.

"Hey, it's her!"

She glanced up and saw a man across the street motioning to his two friends.

"It's the girl who was on the yacht, the one with Jonah Hayes!" the man called out. "Hey, Natalie, did Jonah kick you out?"

She stood poised like a wild animal caught in a hunter's scope. She couldn't believe that someone would recognize her, let alone make such personal remarks. The three men started to cross the street, and by now other people had begun to notice her. She glanced frantically around for a cab and saw one about a block away. Getting a good grip on her suitcase, she whistled the cab down and started jogging toward it. Mercifully the driver saw her and started backing in her direction.

"Don't run away, sweetheart!" called one of the men.

"How about a cup of coffee and a doughnut?" shouted another one. "You'd be safe with me. I know the Heimlich maneuver."

She yanked open the back door of the cab and jumped in, pulling her suitcase with her. "Central Park West."

"Sure thing." The cabbie pulled into traffic before glancing in the rearview mirror at his passenger. "Say, aren't you the one that was on the yacht yesterday? With the fireman who saved your puppy?"

"No."

The cabbie shrugged. "If you say so. But you could be her twin sister. You're even wearing the same kind of clothes she had on. Did you see it on TV?"

"No." Natalie tried to make herself smaller and less conspicuous. When she got home she'd have to burn this outfit. Maybe she'd dye her hair red.

"Well, the two of them were on this fancy boat," the cabbie continued, apparently feeling chatty. "That was part of the prize from that bachelor-auction deal set up by Heart Books, I guess. Anyway, they were eating lunch, and the girl choked on something and this guy saved her with the Heimlich maneuver. True-life drama."

Natalie tried to tune him out. Remembering yesterday inflicted too much pain. Yesterday was B.D., Before the Disaster. Yesterday Jonah was still a hero, her knight in shining armor. Today he was just another schmuck.

"I tell you, my wife just about swooned when she saw how he jumped to that girl's rescue, especially after the puppy episode a few months ago. She said the guy—I think his name is Jonah something—should run for mayor."

Natalie remained silent. At last the cabbie seemed to get the idea that she wasn't interested in conversation and started humming to himself. Natalie closed her eyes and leaned her head against the seat in total exhaustion. She ached all over. An hour ago she hadn't minded the little aches and pains that naturally accompanied a night of almost constant lovemaking. She'd even welcomed the twinges as evidence of time well spent. Now she heartily resented them. Especially the hollow ache in her heart.

NATALIE FORTIFIED HERSELF with a couple of hours' sleep before she went to see her mother. She would rather not go at all, but she'd promised to report in, and if she didn't show up, Alice would be down to check on her. Besides, her mother was keeping Bobo, and Natalie wanted to see her dog. She could use a dose of unconditional love right now.

The minute Alice opened the door, Natalie smelled homemade soup. Her mother hadn't made soup since her father died. The curtains were open and sunlight streamed into the familiar apartment. All evidence of Alice's depression seemed to be gone.

Natalie was determined not to rain on her mother's parade. "Hi, Mom!" she said, avoiding eye contact by dropping to her knees to greet Bobo, who'd hurled himself at her. "How's my boy? Oh, that's a good dog! Did you miss me?"

Panting happily, Bobo rolled to his back to have his tummy scratched. For some reason his exuberance made Natalie want to cry. Not good. She deliberately dragged out the time spent playing with him until she was reasonably sure she was in control of herself.

"Well? Tell me all about it!" her mother said. "I know you two ran away from the Plaza, which was *so* romantic. It gave me another idea for a scene in my book. I've been typing away, having the best time. You and Jonah are a real inspiration for my muse."

A sense of failure nearly overwhelmed Natalie. How could she tell her mother that the romance was over and watch the light go out of Alice's eyes? She hadn't been this animated in ages, and Natalie was about to squelch that glowing spark. Dammit, anyway. The first project to lift her mother's depression might fizzle because Jonah wouldn't cooperate.

"Natalie? You're being awfully quiet. Is anything wrong, sweetheart?"

She couldn't burst her mother's bubble. She just couldn't. Maybe if she bought a little time, she'd figure out what to do. She glanced up from petting Bobo. "It's just that I'm very tired," she said, acting as if the admission embarrassed her a little.

"Ah." Her mother smiled indulgently. "I won't pry into the reasons for *that*. When you left the Plaza, it was obvious to everyone watching, including me, that you two wanted to be alone. I can imagine how exciting that must have been for you, considering how you feel about him."

"Right." Natalie gave Bobo a final pat and stood. The weekend certainly had been exciting. And now she longed to wring a certain fireman's neck. "So the book's going well?"

"It's going great. I've decided to write what I can and hold off on the scenes where I'll need Jonah's help. Do you think he will help me? I can hardly wait to meet him. When will you be seeing him again?"

Her mother's eagerness nearly broke Natalie's heart. "Uh, well, we—"

"Never mind." Alice laid a hand on Natalie's arm. "I'm sure you want to spend time alone at first and really get to know each other. I don't need to barge in at this point and invade your precious privacy. After all, you have a lot at stake. Have you admitted to him about blowing your retirement fund on the auction?"

Natalie's head began to throb. Thirty-three thousand down the drain, not to mention her mother's project in the dumper. "Not yet."

"I'd love to know his reaction. I don't see how he could be anything but flattered that you'd be so reckless in order to be with him."

"I don't know. Jonah's not big on flattery." Now *there* was the understatement of the century.

"I still think he'll be deeply touched, and very impressed. A reporter on the news said that women have been sending bouquets by the dozens to his station. But I'd say your gesture has them all beat."

"I guess so." Natalie thought about all that money. Sure, it had gone for a good cause, and she could take some comfort in that, but her gesture hadn't accomplished what she'd needed it to accomplish. Dammit, she couldn't just let that sacrifice be in vain.

"I need to go check my soup," Alice said, turning to go into the kitchen. "Would you like a bowl, darling? Or are you living on love?"

"I would love a bowl," Natalie said, determined to eat something. She would need her strength to deal with Jonah. Because, in the past few minutes she'd decided that he *was* indeed going to help her mother. She'd just gone about the whole thing wrong. She'd allowed herself to succumb to the attraction between them, and that had been a horrendous mistake.

But she'd learned something about Jonah by spending the evening with his neighbors in the apartment building. He was constitutionally incapable of turning his back on a person in trouble. Alice's depression over the death of her husband had been Natalie's trump card, and she'd let it go to waste. At first she'd been reluctant to reveal the situation until she knew Jonah better, and then she'd been too proud to tell him after he'd insulted both her and her mother's project.

However, pride couldn't figure into this, not when Alice's mental well-being was at stake. She would explain to Jonah why he needed to help her mother, and he would respond. But she had to be very strong about one thing. They must not, under any circumstances, make love again.

11

THE WIG ITCHED and the mustache was on crooked. Natalie sighed and slowly eased the mustache off so she could try again. Never in her wildest dreams had she imagined she'd have to disguise herself so that people wouldn't recognize her on the street. But her picture, along with Jonah's, had been plastered all over the Sunday edition of the *Times*. Besides that, clips of the yacht trip and the escape from the Plaza kept showing up on television.

Just her luck that not much was happening in the city these days, so the media had focused on Jonah's supposed romance with the puppy lady. Natalie felt as if all of Manhattan was preoccupied with her life, and she couldn't believe how she hated it. Her answering machine was filled with messages from people wanting an interview, relationship advice, her hairdresser's name, a lock of her hair, a lock of Bobo's hair. The list seemed endless.

She'd had a taste of this craziness over the weekend, but until Sunday morning, she'd had Jonah's protection to mute the effect. Now she faced the onslaught alone, and she wasn't having a bit of fun. She finally understood the hell he'd been through after Bobo's rescue.

More important than that, she could understand why he'd been so upset, so quick to condemn her when she'd told him about her mother's book. He'd endured this kind of hounding for weeks, until he probably expected everyone he met to want a piece of him. No doubt he'd hoped she was different, but in all honesty, she hadn't been. No wonder he'd snapped.

She would tell him that tonight, assuming she could get her mustache to stay on. According to Mrs. Ruggerelo, Jonah had been on duty at the station but was expected home sometime tonight. Once Natalie had told Mrs. Ruggerelo about her mother's depression and the book project, she'd agreed to let Natalie into the apartment to wait for Jonah.

Natalie had figured out early in the week that she'd have to create a disguise to visit Jonah. She couldn't risk being followed or recognized when she walked into his building. The press already knew where she lived and worked, but her notoriety would fade soon because she was only The Girlfriend, and soon she wouldn't even be considered that. Jonah had to protect himself, though, especially if women got wind of the fact he was free.

Free. The thought of him becoming involved with another woman curdled her insides, so she tried not to think about it. The main thing to remember was that *she* couldn't be involved with him, not if she wanted him to help her mother. And definitely not if he believed the only reason she'd made love to him was to enhance her mother's research.

Finally the mustache seemed glued on straight. One thing was for sure, she was in the right town for disguises. She'd had no trouble finding the wig and mustache, or the oversize trousers, derby hat and dark overcoat. She belted a pillow inside the waistband of the trousers, pulled on the overcoat, put on the derby and left her apartment.

People stared at her as she caught a cab and directed the driver to the Lower East Side, but when she left the cab two blocks from Jonah's apartment and started to walk, no one called out her name. There were a few curious glances, though. For the first time since Sunday morning, she relaxed. Let them think she was a kook, just so no one recognized her.

A light rain fell as she walked, and she turned up her coat collar. She'd been too busy with her disguise to think about the weather and bring an umbrella. At the entrance to Jonah's building, she buzzed the Ruggerelos' apartment.

"Trick or treat," she called into the intercom. "It's Natalie in disguise."

Mrs. Ruggerelo's amused voice came on immediately. "I'll meet you at Jonah's, *cara mia*."

As Natalie climbed the stairs, she remembered how excited she'd been going up these same stairs on Saturday night. And how heartbroken descending them again Sunday morning. Why, oh why, had she allowed herself to be swept along in a wave of passion?

She knew the answer. Jonah, with his intense eyes, generous nature and breathtaking body was irresistible. Approaching his apartment now she felt warm with desire, and he wasn't even there. When he arrived, she'd have to be very strong and show no feeling for him whatsoever.

Mrs. Ruggerelo hurried down the hall from the other direction. When she caught sight of Natalie, she clapped her hand to her mouth and her eyes widened.

Natalie smiled. "What do you think?"

"I think you look like Charlie Chaplin on one of his

bad days." She shook her head. "But I wouldn't have recognized you until you smiled. Or until I looked close at your eyes."

"That was the idea. I didn't want to give away Jonah's location, and with the way people recognize me now, they'd figure it out if they saw me here."

Mrs. Ruggerelo nodded as she put her key in the lock of Jonah's door. "Now you're a celebrity, too."

"And I hate that."

"Well, that's where you and Jonah are alike." She opened the door and went inside, flipping on a light. "Now, I have to warn you, he's in a terrible mood."

Natalie followed. "That's my fault. I handled this business about my mother's book all wrong."

"Could be." Mrs. Ruggerelo stood with her hands on her hips, surveying the apartment. "What a disgrace. He's never left the place like this."

Natalie had to admit the living room was a mess. The Sunday paper was strewn over the floor, as if Jonah had tossed it in a fit of anger. Which he probably had. Half of a sausage pizza sat in its box on the coffee table beside a couple of empty beer bottles. The can of peanuts he'd offered her Saturday night lay halfway across the room, its contents spilled as if it, too, had been the victim of Jonah's fury. And although she distinctly remembered folding his Knicks T-shirt and laying it on top of his dresser, it was in a wadded-up heap on the couch.

Mrs. Ruggerelo glanced at Natalie. "Looks like the boy's in love."

Natalie's jaw dropped. "Are you kidding? He's furious with me."

"Yes, he is." Mrs. Ruggerelo chuckled. "I'm sorry to laugh, but you look so funny in that mustache. I guess you must have stuffed a pillow down your front, too. You look like a pregnant old man."

Natalie glanced down at her bulging middle. "Maybe I overdid it with the pillow, but I didn't want anybody to notice I was a woman."

"I'd love to be a mouse in the corner when Jonah sees you in that getup. Unless you're going to take the mustache and wig off."

"No way. It's too hard to put the mustache back on, and I still have to be disguised when I leave."

"Well, maybe you'll make him laugh and he'll forget how mad he is. And remember that he wouldn't be so upset if he didn't care about you."

Natalie's heart squeezed at the thought, but she pushed the idea away. "If he really cared about me, he wouldn't have accused me of using Saturday night for research on my mother's book."

"I'll bet he didn't really mean that." The little Italian woman leaned down to pick up a section of the newspaper. "You weren't, were you?" She made the question sound casual.

"No!"

"I didn't think so." She picked up another section of the paper and glanced at a picture of Jonah and Natalie fleeing from the Plaza. "Leo argued with me when I told him I was going to let you in. He said you could be making this up about your mother's book. He kept reminding me about that movie *Fatal Attraction* where the bunny gets boiled." She looked up from the newspaper and straight over at Natalie.

"I'm not into boiling bunnies, Mrs. Ruggerelo. Writing a romance is the first thing my mother's been interested in since my father died. Before she got this idea, I was wondering if…if I'd lose them both." She'd never spoken that fear aloud, figuring people would discount it, but it felt very real to her.

Mrs. Ruggerelo nodded in understanding. "It can happen."

Grateful for her empathy, Natalie crouched and gathered the rest of the newspaper from the floor. "Do you think Jonah will believe me when I tell him how important this is and how much I need his help?"

"I've never known him to turn his back on someone in need."

"I'm counting on that."

The older woman surveyed the living room one more time. "But I've never seen him make such a mess of his apartment, either. He's not acting like his usual self these days."

"I don't expect this to be easy," Natalie said. "But whatever happens, I appreciate your help in letting me wait for him in his apartment. I was afraid if I came to his door he wouldn't let me in. But I doubt if he'll throw me out once I'm here. I should get a chance to say my piece."

"Unless he thinks you're a burglar who's climbed in the window. You'd better speak up quick." She chuckled again and handed over the sections of the newspaper she'd picked up. "For your scrapbook."

Natalie made a face.

"Someday you'll want these." Her dark eyes twinkled. "For your bambinos."

JONAH EMERGED from the subway at midnight, bone-weary and convinced that tonight he would finally sleep. The late-afternoon fire had been a hell of a blaze, but what mattered was that they'd put it out and miraculously without casualties. The insurance companies would have huge damage costs, but in Jonah's mind, structural damage was inconsequential if no lives were lost.

The fire had played havoc with everybody's schedule including his, but what the hell. He didn't have anything in particular to get home for. In a way, he dreaded going back to the apartment with its memories of Natalie. His shift at the station had come as a welcome relief, and although he didn't wish fires to happen, fighting this one had worked off a lot of his tension.

He should have cleaned the place before he left for work, should have wiped out all the evidence of her being there so he wouldn't have to face it tonight. But he hadn't, and he was too tired to handle it now. He might end up sleeping on the couch if the pillows on his bed still carried the scent of her perfume. In the morning he'd tackle the job of removing anything that would stir up memories. Thank God he was exhausted and didn't have the energy to miss her right now.

Or so he figured. But when he entered his apartment house and started up the stairs, he remembered the clasp of her hand in his and the brush of that furry white coat. He felt again the perfection of her mouth and saw the surrender in her gray eyes just before they made love. Damn. He'd thought he was too tired to ache like this. Apparently not.

He wanted her to be there in the apartment waiting for him. He imagined the comfort a man could find in her arms after long, punishing hours at a demanding job. And he cursed himself for being a fool. The sooner he gave up that kind of fantasy, the happier he'd be.

When he opened his apartment door he wondered how her special scent could still be there after several days. His imagination must really be playing tricks on him if he—

He stopped in his tracks and stared at the rumpled figure asleep on the couch. Dear God, it was a homeless person. After all his assurances to Natalie that giving out keys was no problem in this building, one of his neighbors had presumed on his good nature and allowed some poor old guy into his apartment on this cold, rain-drenched night.

Jonah had to hope that if a neighbor had let the vagrant in, they'd also decided he was harmless. Although Jonah pitied the poor soul in his ill-fitting clothes, and although he didn't intend to send him out into the cold, he'd sleep better having a conversation with the guy before turning in.

Watching the figure huddled on the couch, he gave the door a shove.

As it slammed shut, the vagrant bolted upright…and his tousled mop of hair shifted.

Jonah's breath caught as familiar gray eyes blinked at him and a lock of blond hair slipped out from under what was obviously a black wig. His heart began to pound. "Natalie?"

"What time is it?"

"After midnight. Natalie, what in God's name are you—"

"Where have you been?"

He blew out a breath. He'd fantasized coming home to the warm welcome of her arms. He hadn't pictured being given the third degree. And he definitely hadn't pictured a mustache. "What are you doing here, and what's up with the disguise?"

"I didn't want anyone to recognize me coming into

your apartment." She touched her mustache. "Is this still straight?"

"Not exactly." He was beginning to absorb the idea that she was here, that she'd deliberately come to see him and that she'd even taken care to protect his privacy. She hadn't answered his question about why she'd come, but he could only think of one reason. She wanted to make amends.

He should be cautious. He should ask a whole lot of questions before desire short-circuited his brain. But damned if he wanted to be cautious. He just wanted her. In his exhausted state, all the reasons why that was a bad idea deserted him, driven away by the thought of holding her, kissing her, being deep inside her again.

"Why don't you take off the mustache now that you're safely here?" He tossed his coat over a chair. "In fact, I'll help you."

"No!" She put a protective hand over the fuzzy thing. "It's too hard to put back on."

He sat down on the couch. "We'll figure something out in the morning." He reached for her. "I wore one of these for Halloween once. I'll bet I can—"

"Don't." She backed away from him. "Please leave my mustache alone. I need it."

"Right this minute?" He gazed at her in bewilderment. "I hate to break it to you, but I've figured out who you are." Damn, but she looked cute, though. He edged closer. "And kissing a woman wearing a mustache doesn't really appeal to me."

"I don't want you to kiss me." She stood up and her pants fell down. "Oh, dear." She grabbed for the pants as a pillow slid out from under her shirt and plopped to the floor. "Everything's coming apart!"

He tried not to laugh. "Does it matter?"

"Of course it matters! It took me forever to get this arranged, and now I'll have to do it all over again." She pulled up her pants. Clutching a handful of the material to keep the trousers up, she started to reach for the pillow on the floor.

He grasped her wrist. "I figure you'll have to do it all over again, anyway," he said quietly.

She looked into his eyes and sucked in her breath, making her mustache flutter.

He couldn't help grinning at the picture she made. He might be willing to work his way around that mustache, after all, if she was so hell-bent on keeping it. He stroked the inside of her wrist with his thumb. "Don't tell me you disguised yourself and came all the way over here in the middle of the night just to talk."

Her heated gaze said she wanted him, but she pulled away from his grip. "As a matter of fact, I did."

"You just want to talk." He couldn't believe it. Maybe this was another game. He forced himself to lean back against the couch, willing his raging hormones to settle down. "About what?"

She abandoned the pillow and sat down at the far end of the couch. "There's something I didn't tell you Sunday morning."

He braced himself. For a woman who was so open and honest in his bed, she sure had a lot of secrets out of it. "Such as?"

"After my father died, my mother became very depressed."

"That makes sense. You said they were married a long time."

She fixed him with a piercing gaze. "No, I mean *very* depressed. She took no interest in anything, wouldn't get dressed, barely ate. Her only activity was putting together jigsaw puzzles, and the pieces began to peel because she'd cry the whole time she worked on them."

She had his attention now. Briefly he considered she could be making all this up, but she'd have to be one hell of an actress to fake her concern as she described her mother's condition. Besides, the detail about the jigsaw puzzles wasn't something a person would include in a lie.

"I tried everything," she continued. "In fact, Bobo was one of my failed experiments. I ended up taking him to live with me because she wasn't giving him anything more than the basics. Then when you saved him from the lake, she commented that you'd make a good romance hero."

He was afraid that's where she was headed with this story. He got an uneasy feeling in the pit of his stomach. "So you said."

"I didn't think anything about it, but a week or so later she told me she'd started writing a book. She hasn't let me read it, but I've seen the stack of pages. More than that, I saw the change in her. It was miraculous, Jonah."

As he felt the trap closing, he tried to find a way out. "So it's her first try at something like this?"

"Her first serious try."

"Then I don't suppose there's much chance she'll get the book published."

"Oh, there's an excellent chance. She's a good writer. Unfortunately for her talent, my father was a literary critic for the *Times*. After she saw the way he ripped apart books by well-known writers, she didn't dare finish her own novel and submit it for publication. She swore me to secrecy, so I don't think he ever knew about her dreams."

Jonah shook his head. "That's too bad."

"But understandable. I loved my dad, but he was an intellectual snob who didn't think a book was any good unless it had a dismal ending. My mother liked romances with happy endings. She and my dad had a running argument about whether escapist fiction had any place in literature. What I'm saying is that she knows publishing because of my father, and she knows the romance market from her own reading."

"Oh." Jonah felt that door slam and searched for another. "Listen, I'm sure there are lots of guys down at my station who would love to help her. I can give you several names. I'm sure the chief would cooperate." He'd relish getting the chief involved, come to think of it. The chief owed him.

"I tried to convince her of that." She gazed at him. "But it's as if you're her talisman, Jonah. She seems to believe that a connection to you will give her book the spark it needs to get published."

The knot in his stomach tightened. "So that's why you spent thirty-three thousand dollars on me."

"Yes, but—"

He held up a hand. "The yes part is enough for now. Why didn't you tell me all about your mother from the beginning?"

"I should have."

"Yes, you should have. That first night in the cab, you should have spilled the whole story." And he never would have kissed her, he thought. He'd thought her motivation was to be with him, and he'd been turned on to that, no matter how much he'd tried to deny it and make fun of her extravagance. Instead, she'd spent the money for her mother, not because she'd lusted after him. That made all the difference.

"I wanted to get to know you first," she said. "My mother's very vulnerable right now. Harsh criticism could stop her in her tracks, so I had to make sure you weren't the kind of guy who would make fun of her efforts."

"And getting to know me included sleeping with me?" Anger sharpened his tone, but he couldn't help it.

"I didn't mean for that to happen."

"There's a very effective way you could have stopped it. You could have said no."

"I should have." Her voice dropped to a whisper. "I was very selfish." She looked down at her lap and murmured something else.

"I didn't catch that."

She glanced up, her eyes brimming with misery. "I was having too good a time! So I sacrificed my mother's project because I couldn't bear to take a chance that when I told you, you wouldn't make love to me."

He was across the couch immediately and took her by the arms. "Then it wasn't all part of the plan? You made love to me because you wanted to?"

"How can you even ask?"

"Oh, Natalie." Just as he'd decided to kiss her, mustache and all, she wiggled away from him and scrambled off the couch.

"But we're not doing it again!" she said, backing away.

"Why the hell not?"

"Because this time I'm here because of my mother. And all I want to know is whether you'll help her."

She was like a dog with a bone, and he might as well face this thing. "Will she make sure that I'm not recognizable as the hero?"

"I promise she will. I'll make sure of it. After what I've been through in the past few days, I really understand your position on that."

"Then I'll help her."

Natalie's face lit up like the Fourth of July. "Thank you, Jonah."

He stood and started toward her. "And now that I've agreed to help, would you please take off that mustache?"

"No." Her eyes darkened with regret. "Because we're not making love. It can only mess things up. I don't want you to think I'm taking mental notes for my mother's book, and you could easily think that and abandon the whole program. I'm not taking that chance."

She had a point. But he didn't want to acknowledge it when it would mean not making love to her tonight or any night in the near future. "Listen, Natalie—"

"Will you still help, even if I don't go to bed with you?"

That got him. "Of course! What sort of guy do you think I am?"

"Thank you, Jonah. I'm very, very grateful. Oh, there's one other thing. I've told my mother that I bid on you because I was crazy about you. So now she thinks that we're sweethearts. Your helping her is only a by-product of us being lovers."

"So I'm not supposed to touch you, but as far as your mother knows, we're going at it hot and heavy?"

"That's right."

He passed a hand over his face. He must be insane to get involved with this crazy deal. "Okay."

"Great. As soon as I get the pillow fixed right and the wig straight, I'm leaving."

"The hell you say! I'm not letting you wander around out there by yourself at one o'clock in the morning."

She paused, as if she hadn't thought about that situation. "I'd planned for it to be earlier when I went home. Why are you so late?"

"A fire. It took a lot of us to get it out."

Her gray eyes clouded. "Are you okay?"

"Tired, but okay. You're staying here until morning, Natalie. I don't want any argument on that. You're so worried about your mother. How would she react to knowing you were out alone in that crazy disguise at this hour?"

"You're right." She sighed. "But if I stay, we can't make love. I've thought it all through, and I'm sure it's the right decision. Please help me keep my promise to myself."

He groaned. She knew exactly how to get to him. "Then take my bed tonight. I'll sleep on the couch."

"The couch is fine for me."

"No, it's not. There's no door on the couch."

"But—"

"*Natalie.*"

"Okay, okay." She started toward the bedroom.

He watched her toddle back there in her strange get-up and he ached to go with her. But she didn't want him to. He hated thinking she might be right about this, but he had a suspicion she could be. He wouldn't want to think about her mother's book while he made love to her, but he probably would anyway, and he'd wonder if everything they did would end up in print. "Lock the door," he said.

She nodded and kept going.

12

NATALIE RATED IT the worst night of her life. She took off the wig, coat and trousers and slept in her shirt. The mustache drove her crazy, but the worst part was lying in the bed where she'd made such wonderful love with Jonah. At least twenty times during the night she left the bed and started to unlock the door.

It was an old lock and required some wiggling, and after she'd struggled with it for a couple of seconds she'd come to her senses and remember why she must not go to Jonah. He'd agreed to help her mother. That fragile gift was balanced on a narrow ledge, and any sort of motion on her part could cause it to fall and shatter. With a sigh she'd go back to his bed to toss and turn for another hour.

At dawn she got dressed. The pillow was in the living room, so she decided not to bother incorporating it into her costume. She tightened her belt to cinch up the waist of the trousers as best she could. Once she got the wig on, it looked okay, but the mustache had a bad case of bed-head, with one side smashed like an accordion. She tugged and patted before finally giving up and creeping out into the living room.

The sight of Jonah looking cramped and uncomfortable as he lay asleep on the couch nearly undid her. He'd used his jacket as an inadequate blanket, and her pillow was under his head. She fought the urge to go over and kiss his unshaven cheek, but that would lead to more complications.

She should never have made love to him in the first place. There must have been a point before they'd climbed into bed Saturday night when she'd known he could be trusted with her mother's project. She could have asked him then and avoided all this mutual frustration and pain. But she hadn't recognized that point and once it was gone, passion had taken over.

She decided to leave the pillow, not trusting herself to wake him up. She found a pad of paper and a pencil by the telephone in the kitchen and wrote down her mother's name, address and telephone number. She hesitated, wondering what else to write. Finally she scribbled *thank you* and signed her name.

Tiptoeing into the living room again, she left the pad of paper on the coffee table and leaned down to pick up her derby from where it had fallen on the floor beside the couch.

His hand shot out and grabbed her with such suddenness that she lost her balance and he pulled her easily to her knees beside him. "Going somewhere?"

Her heart thumped rapidly at the dark intensity in his eyes. "Home," she murmured.

His grip tightened. "Without saying goodbye?"

"I didn't want to wake you."

"Liar." He reached up and cupped the back of her head as he studied her expression. "You were afraid to wake me."

"Okay, I was afraid. Afraid of this."

"Hey." His lazy grin belied the fire in his eyes. "You don't have to be afraid of me."

"I'm not." Her heartbeat quickened to the familiar

rhythm it had learned in response to Jonah. "I'm afraid of me."

"Your mustache looks like a caterpillar that ran headfirst into a wall."

"I know."

"So a little more mashing can't hurt, right?"

"Jonah—"

"I've been wondering all night long what it would be like to kiss a woman wearing a mustache."

"No. It's a bad idea." She tried to pull away.

His fingers splayed across the back of her head and held her firmly. "Your wig feels like steel wool and that coat smells of mothballs. God knows why you turn me on all decked out like this, but you do. I probably need a shrink."

"We probably both do. Jonah, let me go."

"I'm not going to seduce you." His gaze probed hers. "I just want a kiss before you go. After this morning, I won't be allowed."

Flames of desire licked away at her resolve. "You know we won't stop with a kiss."

"Yes, we will. I promise." He released her wrist and lifted his hand to stroke his knuckles across her cheek. "Because you're right about making love while your mother's writing this book. It's not a good idea."

She closed her eyes and leaned into his gentle caress, needy as a kitten. She shouldn't feel disappointed that he agreed with her. She shouldn't, but she did. "No, it's not a good idea."

His voice grew husky as he continued to brush his knuckles over her skin. "How long will it take her to finish it?"

"I have no idea."

"Weeks?"

"Probably." She sighed. His touch felt so good.

"Months?"

"I hope not."

"That's my girl." He guided her gently down. Trying various angles, he finally muttered an oath and slid one finger under the bottom of the mustache to lift it away from her upper lip. "Now I know why women complain about these things," he murmured.

She couldn't imagine how this kiss could turn out well, but somehow he managed to capture her mouth and slide his finger away in one amazingly coordinated movement. And once he finally connected, she forgot about the mustache, and her disguise, and her mother, and her mother's book. His lips moving against hers instantly brought back the powerful need that had swept her into his arms and into his bed. Nothing else existed but that driving passion.

The thrust of his tongue flooded her with heat and moisture. She didn't even realize she was unfastening the buttons of his shirt until he caught her hand and pressed it flat against his chest. His heart thundered underneath her palm.

Slowly she lifted her mouth away from his. "Sorry."

"Don't be."

She raised herself enough to look into his eyes. That didn't help.

Holding her gaze, he brought her hand up to his lips and kissed her palm.

The moist caress made her close her eyes and fight for control. Another few seconds and she'd beg him to make love to her. "I have to go."

"Yeah." His voice was thick with desire. He released her hand and smoothed her mustache with one finger.

"This has been fun, but next time I'd like to try it without the soup-strainer."

Next time. "I think...the only way this will work is...if we don't touch anymore, at least until..."

"I know." He sighed. "But this celibacy thing sounded a whole lot easier ten minutes ago."

She opened her eyes. He lay there all sexy and rumpled, with his shirt half undone and his gaze hot. Somehow she'd have to find the strength to stand up and walk out of this apartment. "I shouldn't have kissed you."

He brushed his knuckle over her lower lip. "Maybe not, but I'm glad you did. Now I know that Saturday night wasn't just a fluke."

"A fluke?" She stared at him in amazement. "Jonah, we made love all night!" And now she wanted to make love all day.

"And then you walked out. I figured you could live without me."

"But last night I told you that I'd let myself forget about my mother's project because I was so desperate to make love to you."

He smiled. "I know, but then you stayed in the bedroom all night long. I didn't really believe you until just now, when you started unbuttoning my shirt."

Her cheeks grew warm with embarrassment. "And I was the one who laid down the ground rules. I don't know what I was thinking."

"Oh, I do," he said softly. "And I loved it. You see, once upon a time I thought you were so hot for my body that you'd bid tons of money to be with me. When I discovered that wasn't what you'd paid for, I felt like a fool for the way I'd come on to you. I wondered if you'd have even been attracted to me if I hadn't put the idea in your head."

She hadn't really thought about the blow his ego had taken when she'd told him her real motivation for bidding on him at the auction. She smiled, remembering how she'd reacted to her first physical contact with him. "You didn't put the idea in my head. I began wanting you the night of the auction when you were squashed in between me and Barb at the table. I fought it. Then I…lost the fight."

"But now, for who knows how long, you're going to win that fight?"

"Yep." Taking a deep breath she stood. "My mother's mental health is at stake. I won't rush her, and I won't take a chance on making love to you and lousing everything up."

He gazed at her. "Let's hope your mother's a fast writer."

WHEN STAN THE DOORMAN caught sight of Natalie getting out of a cab and approaching her apartment building, his eyebrows disappeared beneath the bill of his cap.

"It's me—Natalie," she said.

Stan looked closer before starting to chuckle. "You're losing that disguise, you know."

"I know. But it served its purpose. Now I have to get upstairs and take Bobo for a walk before he messes on the rug."

"Right." He grinned as he held the door for her. "They've tried to interview me, too. Wanted to know about your comings and goings."

Natalie paused. "Really?"

"I pretended not to know who you were."

Natalie's throat tightened with gratitude at his unexpected protectiveness. She'd assumed the people in her building were more distant and uncaring than the ones in Jonah's apartment, but maybe that was because she'd been distant, too.

She laid a hand on Stan's uniformed arm. "Thank you," she said. "That means a lot to me."

"You're welcome."

As Natalie rode the elevator to her floor, she wondered how many women very much like Mrs. Ruggerelo lived in the building, and how many Pete Hornaceks she might find if she opened her eyes. Then she wondered how many of them would have been happy to help her with her mother, had she been willing to ask. The idea had never occurred to her. She'd shouldered the burden alone because that's the way her family had always handled things, but obviously she'd needed help. Without Jonah's cooperation she'd be looking at complete failure.

On her way down the hall, she passed an elderly lady she'd noticed many times, someone who obviously lived on her floor. "Nice morning," she said, smiling at the woman.

"Yes, it is." The woman looked at Natalie as if she had horns and a tail.

Natalie started to label the woman as unfriendly until she remembered her disguise. Maybe now wasn't the time to chat up the neighbors, after all.

It also wasn't the best time to run into her mother, who was presently heading toward Natalie's door at a furious clip.

Alice glanced at Natalie and did a double take. "Is that *you?*"

"Hi, Mom." Natalie took off her derby and pulled off her wig. Ah, much better.

"Natalie Michelle LeBlanc, what *are* you up to? And where have you been? I called your apartment until midnight and started in again at six. Finally I decided to come down and use my key to make sure you were all right, although you know how I hesitate to invade your privacy. I would never use this key unless I thought—"

"It's okay, Mom." Natalie had changed some of her opinions about this privacy business in the past few days. "I'm sorry if I worried you. I should have told you I was spending the night at Jonah's."

"Like that?"

"I didn't want to be recognized going into his apartment building. So far nobody has figured out where he lives, exactly, but if they saw me, they might put two and two together, so I disguised myself." She hurried to unlock the door. Bobo was going crazy barking and whining on the other side. As he leaped at her, she wondered if she could possibly get him outside fast enough, considering that she needed to change clothes and remove her mustache.

"Jonah must have gotten quite a laugh out of seeing you like that," Alice said.

"Oh, yeah, he was hysterical." Natalie glanced at her mother and noticed she was dressed. "Mom, could you please borrow one of my coats and take Bobo for a walk? I'm sure he's desperate and I'd rather not go back out on Central Park West in broad daylight looking like this."

"Sure...in fact, if you weren't here, I'd planned to take him over to the park, like I did this past weekend. He really likes that."

"Yes, he does." Natalie opened her front hall closet and took out a jacket, Bobo's leash and the pooper-scooper while Bobo pranced around frantically. "Thanks, Mom. This is a big help. Just keep a tight grip on the leash."

"Oh, I don't know." Her mother's eyes sparkled. "Bobo's accident seems to have worked out pretty well for you. Be back in a jiffy." Her mother headed down the hall with Bobo pulling on the leash.

Natalie stood in the doorway and watched them go as another revelation hit her. Perhaps she'd been so hell-bent on doing things for her mother that she hadn't considered that Alice might need to do things for her. She hadn't asked anything of her mother since her father had died until the weekend she'd spent with Jonah, when she'd needed her to take care of Bobo.

She thought about Jonah's neighbors. No one took without giving back, even Mrs. Sanchez, who crocheted baby clothes for the triplets. Jonah, Leo and Pete had made sure Beth got to the hospital in time, and she'd named each of them a godfather to one of her sons. Everything was based on give-and-take.

Uneasiness stabbed her as she realized how much Jonah was giving to her and Alice by agreeing to help with the book. And what could she give him in return? Certainly not what he wanted the most, although it was the very gift she longed to give. Something else, then. She'd have to think about it.

THE FIRST NIGHT Jonah agreed to pay a visit to Alice LeBlanc, a downpour drenched Manhattan. Jonah considered it good luck, because people were so busy staying out of the rain they didn't bother to notice him. The doorman at Natalie's apartment recognized him, but otherwise he made it to Alice's door without causing any comment.

He took off his raincoat, ran a hand through his damp hair and rang the bell. Alice had said Natalie didn't want to interfere with the interview, so she'd planned to go to the movies with her friend Barb. According to Alice, Natalie had said she'd see him later on. He doubted it.

In fact, now that a couple of days had gone by and he was faced with the life-style Natalie enjoyed on Central Park West, all his old insecurities about her had resurfaced. He believed that she wanted him to help her mother, but he'd begun to doubt that she wanted him—at least on any long-term basis.

Maybe she'd allowed herself to get carried away a few times when he was right there to tempt her. After all, they were two healthy people with normal sex drives, and they'd been placed in a seductive situation. But he was afraid that with Natalie, the urge faded the minute he was out of sight. She'd never mentioned missing him when they were apart, so maybe she didn't ache the way he did every time he thought about the night they'd shared.

The door opened and Alice LeBlanc beamed at him. He recognized Natalie's delicate features traced with the fine lines of middle age. Her hair was short like Natalie's but salt-and-pepper instead of blond. Blue eyes gazed at him instead of the soft gray that haunted his dreams, but the smile was so much like Natalie's that his breath hitched. Alice was a lovely woman, as he expected Natalie would be when she reached her fifties. And God help him, he wanted to be there.

"You must be Jonah." Alice held out both hands. "How wonderful to meet you at last."

He took her hands in his—warm hands that reminded him of his mother's. He'd somehow expected a society matron's grasp to be different, cooler and more perfunctory. Beth was right. He needed to work on his prejudices. "Same here, Mrs. LeBlanc."

"Alice," she corrected, drawing him inside and shutting door. "Unless you'd rather call me Mom?"

He nearly choked.

She looked at him with concern. "Oh, dear, did I overstep? Maybe I'm making assumptions I shouldn't make about you two, but considering the way Natalie feels, I thought—"

"I'm crazy about your daughter," he found himself saying. It wasn't hard to admit the truth. "But we haven't actually started talking about a future together."

"I see. Here, let me take your coat." She hooked it over an antique coat tree in the hall. "Come and sit down. I made coffee. I thought you might like some after ploughing through this nasty weather."

"Sounds great."

"Make yourself comfortable. I'll get the coffee."

He walked into the living room but he didn't sit down right away. There was too much to see. The apartment smelled of lemon oil, which also reminded him of his mother, and to be honest, the furniture didn't look any more expensive than what he'd grown up with. The rain-soaked view of Central Park and the glittering lights on Fifth Avenue were the only thing that separated this room from its counterpart in Buffalo, but it was still a big distinction.

A bookcase covered one wall, and framed family pictures were scattered among the leather-covered volumes. He homed in on the pictures, greedy for information about Natalie's childhood. What struck him about the pictures, considering that he was used to seeing family photos crammed with faces, was how few people were in the photo gallery of a family with an only child. He studied the serious look in Natalie's father's eyes and understood why he'd intimidated Natalie's mother so much. But the guy had missed knowing something important about his wife, which hadn't been fair to either of them.

Then he picked up a picture of Natalie looking full of vinegar as she modeled her Brownie uniform, and he smiled. He could just picture her chasing Jimmy Holcomb around the playground.

"I consider it a very good sign when a man starts looking at a woman's family pictures," Alice said as she set a tray on the coffee table.

Jonah replaced the picture of Natalie and turned to face her. "And why's that?"

"It indicates you're interested in her as a person, not just as a sex object."

Jonah coughed into his fist. "Is that so?" he managed to say at last.

"Well, I'm right, aren't I?"

"Yes, you're right." The truth was, he wondered if Natalie was interested in *him* only as a sex object, but he didn't think that was the right comment to make to her mother.

Alice smiled and gestured toward the couch. A yellow legal pad, a pen and a small tape recorder lay on the lamp table beside her. "I'm so glad you've turned out to be the person Natalie hoped you'd be."

He walked over and sat down while she poured them each a mug of coffee from an insulated carafe very much like one his mother owned. If he'd expected bone china, he wasn't going to get it. Another assumption bit the dust. "And who do you think she hoped I'd be?" he asked.

Alice gave him a confidential glance. "Well, by now you must realize a woman like Natalie wouldn't spend that kind of money on a one-night stand."

No, but she'd spend it to save her mother, and the one-night stand might have been a bonus. "I realize that, but she was also helping a worthy cause, don't forget."

"That was a nice extra, but I'm here to tell you that Natalie doesn't love the cause of literacy thirty-three thousand dollars' worth. She was after you."

He picked up his coffee and took a bracing sip. He might as well make use of this chance to get some information out of this woman. She certainly wasn't pulling any punches with him. "I'll be honest with you, Alice. I still have trouble believing that someone with Natalie's money, the kind of money that allowed her to bid on me at the auction, would be interested in a future with a guy who fights fires for a living."

The light of battle came into Alice's blue eyes, and her tone became more aggressive. "You don't know Natalie as well as I thought you would by now if you'd make a statement like that. Money, or the lack of it, would be the last thing she'd consider in a relationship."

He felt properly chastised. "Point taken. And I'm sorry. It's just that..." He searched for the right words. "If you can try to put yourself in my shoes, a guy like me can't even imagine how someone could just write out a check for that amount when it's not for a car, or a down payment on a house, or somebody's college fund. It's almost unreal to me."

"I told you she didn't do it lightly."

"No, but the point is she did it." He gazed at her. "I can't relate to a gesture like that, but that's probably because to me, it would be such a big deal."

"And you think it was ostentatious," Alice said.

"In a way, yeah. I'm sorry if you take that wrong. Natalie's a terrific person and I'm sure she meant well. But to be perfectly honest, that's how it seems to me."

Alice sighed. "That girl. I told her she should confess, but I can see she hasn't, and so your opinion of her is suffering as a result. That's no way to run a love affair."

Another confession. Jonah didn't know if he was up to it.

"I need to ask you something, and you must search your heart and answer me as honestly as you can."

Jonah put down his coffee mug. "All right."

"You mentioned that you were worried about the money angle of your relationship. Is that because, if the conditions were reversed and you had more money than your sweetheart, you'd consider that a problem?"

"Of course not!"

"I didn't think so." Alice gave him a smug smile. "Men usually can't see it the other way around."

"If you're trying to get me to be fair, I've tried very hard to do that. I'll keep trying. It's just that—"

"I'm trying to get you to see my little girl for the impetuous, lovable person she is," Alice said. "I'm afraid by the time you discover the truth it may be too late." She took both of his hands in hers. "If I tell you something, you must promise to keep it to yourself. Natalie's pride's getting in her way, and I can't stand by and watch that happen. Will you promise?"

Jonah couldn't imagine what was coming next, but he looked into Alice's eyes and promised anyway.

"Natalie and I aren't very well off. Our two apartments are rent controlled because of an old agreement with my uncle, who used to own the building. Natalie's still struggling to make a go of stocks, and I'm managing with the income from a small life-insurance policy on my husband because I'm not old enough for social security. Neither one of us has spare cash."

Jonah stared at her. "Then how did she pay for me at the auction?"

"She emptied her retirement fund for you, Jonah."

13

"YOU'RE KIDDING," Jonah said, grappling with what Alice had told him.

"No, I'm not." She squeezed his hands and released them. "But you can't say anything. She's convinced you'll think it was a stupid move on her part, and she wouldn't appreciate my telling you. But for the future of your relationship, I felt I had to."

Jonah took a deep breath. "Okay, let me understand. She had a retirement account, but she had other savings, right? I mean, that was just one of her—" He stopped speaking as Alice slowly shook her head. "You're telling me she wiped out all her savings?" Jonah hoped he had the wrong idea.

"Yes. And I must say it's typical. When she was a kid, she had a coin collection. We saved old nickels, dimes and pennies for her and some of them were quite rare. When she was fourteen years old, she wanted to buy us a special Christmas present, so she spent them. She didn't even take them to a coin dealer—just put them right into a clerk's hands to be used at face value."

Jonah wasn't really surprised at the story. Suddenly all the aspects of Natalie's personality made sense to him, and he was happy to know the depth of her generosity.

However...she hadn't told him about her sacrifice.

In many little ways, she'd let him continue to think she was wealthy enough to afford the auction bid. Maybe it was her pride, as her mother had said. But after seeing the way he'd put himself out for his neighbors, how could she think he'd condemn her?

Unfortunately, there could be another reason that she hadn't told him. If he knew she was his financial equal, there would be no barriers left between them. And maybe, just maybe, she wanted to keep those barriers. Sure, the sex was great, but that didn't mean she wanted a lifetime commitment.

"You're thinking so hard I can hear the wheels turning," Alice said. "Please tell me you aren't going to judge Natalie for such a wildly romantic impulse."

"Only a fool would do that," Jonah said, earning him a brilliant smile from Alice. "But it changes things, knowing the truth about the auction."

"Good. I couldn't have you believing my girl is a show-off."

Jonah picked up his coffee mug. "When she cashed in her coin collection, what did she buy you and her father?"

"A beautiful edition of *Pride and Prejudice*. She said a teacher at school had told her the romance novel had its roots in Jane Austen's books, which are now considered classics, of course. I guess she was trying to tell me something—or maybe it was her father she wanted to tweak. She's always been supportive of my writing."

But she hadn't given her husband a chance to be, Jonah thought. Just as Natalie wasn't giving Jonah a chance to be supportive about blowing her retirement money. "Natalie believes in you," he said. "That's why she asked me to help."

"And I appreciate that help."

"I'm glad to do it, as long as nobody recognizes me as the hero in the book."

Alice grimaced. "Natalie has made that very clear. Now that she knows what it's like to be hounded, she doesn't want to make your life even more miserable than she has already."

"You know, all things considered, it's been worth it." And it had been, even if it turned out that Natalie was only playing him for a fool, even if he never held her in his arms again. He wouldn't trade the night they'd spent together for anything, not even the privacy he used to love.

"I'm so glad to hear you say that." Alice reached for the legal pad and the tape recorder. "And now I guess we'd better get some work done. Natalie may want to see some results when she gets home."

"When will she be home?"

Alice looked surprised. "You don't know? I figured you two would have decided to meet down at her place after you were finished here."

Jonah thought quickly. Alice thought they were hot-and-heavy lovers, according to Natalie. Lovers wouldn't miss such an opportunity to spend time together. Come to think of it, he didn't want to miss the opportunity, if only to be near her for a few minutes.

"We planned to get together," he said, "but she wasn't sure which movie Barb wanted to see the last time we talked. I guess she thought you'd fill me in on her plans."

"Oh. Well, last I heard, they were going to a film festival that could take three or four hours." She glanced at her watch. "That's past my bedtime. You wouldn't mind waiting in her apartment, would you?"

"Nope." If Natalie could weasel her way into his

apartment through Mrs. Ruggerelo, then he could certainly justify getting into Natalie's through her mother. His pulse quickened at the prospect. "The problem is she hasn't had time to get a key made for me."

"Oh, that's no problem. I can let you in."

"Great." Better than great, he thought as an idea slowly took shape. Alice had been relieved that he didn't view Natalie as merely a sex object. It was suddenly very important to him that Natalie didn't view him as one, either. And he had a plan.

"That's settled, then." Alice switched on the tape recorder. "Now tell me, did you have a happy childhood?"

THE FOREIGN FILMS were obscure, but Natalie didn't think she would have been able to concentrate no matter what Barb had suggested seeing. Thinking of her mother and Jonah having a long conversation gave her a headache. She'd achieved her goal, and now all she could imagine was disaster. Both of them held a different piece of her secret, and bringing them together might really cook her goose.

Twice during the evening she'd been recognized, once as she and Barb bought their tickets and again as they waited for a cab to take them home. Both times Natalie was able to turn aside the prying questions and escape, but she hated the idea that every time she appeared in public she had to worry about this sort of intrusion. Barb thought it was funny, but then Barb didn't have to live through it, either.

By the time Natalie walked down the hall to her apartment, unbuttoning her raincoat as she walked, her nerves were raw. She fit the key in the lock and heard Bobo's tags jangling as he pranced around on the other side of the door. Petting him would help, she thought. She'd play with him for a while until she calmed down enough to get some sleep.

She opened the door and he frisked around her, as always. She leaned down to rub his head, but he darted away and ran into the living room. She followed, and immediately gave a little yelp of surprise.

Jonah was sprawled casually on the couch, an unreadable look in his dark eyes as he gazed at her. "Can I take your coat?"

A million thoughts raced through her mind as all the disasters she'd imagined happening during the evening became distinct possibilities. But overriding her concern was another, more elemental reaction. Jonah in a casual knit shirt and jeans lounging on her living-room couch was a very provocative sight indeed.

On Saturday night he'd offered to take her coat, too, and that had been the beginning of the most incredible evening of her life. She clenched her hands against the urge to hold them out, to invite him to touch, to stroke, to do whatever came naturally.

She cleared her throat. "What...why are you...how did you..."

He scratched behind Bobo's ears. It was obvious he'd already become Bobo's fast friend. "Your mother let me in."

"Why?" The obvious reason made her tremble.

He gave Bobo a final pat and got up from the couch. "She assumed we'd want to see each other tonight."

Oh, she'd wanted to see him, all right. And now she wanted a whole lot more than visual stimulation. But it wasn't a good idea. "You could have made some excuse."

"I could have, but I didn't want to." He came closer.

Bobo trotted over and insinuated himself between them. "Go lie down," Jonah said.

Natalie watched in amazement as Bobo did as he was told. Something about Jonah's manner was different tonight, she thought. He seemed calmer, more sure of himself. It was very sexy.

"Jonah...I don't know what you—"

"You've told your mother that we're lovers, right?"

"But I didn't give her any details! Please, you have to believe that I won't tell her anything personal about Saturday night."

"I hope to hell you won't, but that's not what I wanted to talk to you about. Your mother's a sharp woman."

Natalie was glad to hear the respect in his voice. Apparently he hadn't managed to insult her mother or her book. She relaxed enough to take off her raincoat and lay it over a nearby chair. "So you got along with each other, then?"

"Sure. Although, as much as she wants to know about me, I wonder how she's going to disguise this hero of hers. I've made her promise to let me read the book before she sends it to anyone."

"That's good. Then you'll know for sure I didn't give away any details of a...sensitive nature." She needed to get off this arousing topic, and fast. "Were you able to help her with the specifics of firefighting?"

"We didn't even get to that. I'll have to come back, maybe more than once, as slow as this process seems to be going. And that's what I think we need to work out. If you keep telling her we're involved, but every time I'm around you scurry off to the movies, eventually she's going to wonder what's up."

She had trouble thinking when he was so close. This

plan had seemed logical at one time, but now the logic was unraveling in the heat of his stare. "I explained that I didn't want to interfere," she said. "The two of you will be working when you're here, after all."

"That's fine as far as it goes, but she thinks we're headed toward the altar. She thinks we're…in love."

She wished he hadn't seemed so hesitant when he said the word. She wondered if the truth of her feelings was sticking out all over her. "So what's your point?"

His gaze intensified. "If we were in love, we'd be together every possible minute. We'd spend the night together whenever we could, at my apartment or yours, because we wouldn't be able to get enough of each other."

Her trembling resumed as she imagined them doing exactly that. "So we'll tell her you're spending the night, even if you don't."

"She'll see through a lie in no time, being as close as she is. Besides, you're an only child. You get all the attention, for better or worse."

She hated to admit he might have a point. Maybe there was a flaw in her plan. But fixing that flaw could endanger the whole scheme.

"There's something else," he said. "She's already mentioned having us both come to dinner some night and I'm supposed to discuss that with you."

"My goodness." Natalie hadn't envisioned this at all. She thought Jonah could just show up, help her mother and then disappear. She'd tell Alice they were seeing each other constantly and life was great, and that would suffice.

"And besides that," Jonah continued, "a guy in love would suggest some activities with his girl and her folks once in a while." His smile was faint. "It's the PC thing to do."

She folded her arms as an unpleasant thought occurred to her. "You seem to be a real expert on this subject of how a man behaves in such situations."

He studied her quietly. "I've been in love before, if that's what you're getting at."

Now, *there* was an unwelcome piece of information. "And that's...how everything went?"

"Approximately."

"And then what?"

"I'm not sure what you mean."

She was growing very ill-tempered, and she knew it. "You're not with her now, are you? What happened after you spent every spare minute together and had all sorts of happy little gatherings with her family?"

His glance was speculative. "Is that important?"

"Yes. No!" She hugged herself tighter and looked away. "Never mind. It's none of my business, is it?"

"I wouldn't say that. About a year ago we decided...that we wanted different things from life. So we went our separate ways."

"And do you still love her?" Whoops. She really shouldn't have asked that.

A light flared in his eyes. He'd caught her slip, and now he could question her about it, if he wanted to see her squirm. "No," he said softly.

Her pulse leaped.

He moved in close, until she could smell his aftershave and feel the heat of his body. She needed to get him out of here before she forgot herself.

"There's so much we don't know about each other." He cupped her cheek. "We've explored every inch of each other's bodies, yet you don't have some basic information about me."

His soft caress was heaven. Slowly she dropped her defensive stance and unfolded her arms. "Such as?"

He stroked her cheekbone with his thumb as he looked deep into her eyes. "I wouldn't have been able to make love to you the way I did on Saturday night if I loved someone else."

Her heart hammered. "Some people take a new lover to forget an old one."

"That's not my style." His mouth tightened. "But I don't know that about you. Were you trying to forget someone?"

"No," she whispered.

His mouth eased into a gentle smile. "Good."

That smile brought her attention to his lips, and she moistened her own, as if she could taste him still, after all these days apart. Then she lifted her gaze to his eyes, and found a warmth there that made her quiver with longing. She envied the woman he'd loved, and wondered if she'd ever felt that intensity of emotion herself. She couldn't remember being obsessed with a man the way he'd described being obsessed with his girlfriend. *Until now.*

As he stroked her cheek, his breathing quickened, and she thought he would kiss her—hoped he would kiss her. As always, her resolve was turning to Silly Putty the longer he dangled temptation in her way.

"So how do you want to handle this?" he asked softly.

She was so dazed and needy that she had no idea what he was talking about. She swallowed. "I'm sorry. I seem to have lost track of what we were discussing."

The flame of desire danced in his eyes, but he just

kept stroking her cheek and made no move to take her in his arms. "We have to figure out how we're going to convince your mother that we're lovers when we're not."

She couldn't remember exactly why they couldn't just *be* lovers. It had something to do with—oh yes, he would think she might tell her mother everything they did in bed and it would appear in the book. It was about trust.

"I guess you're still afraid that anything that happens between us will be repeated to my mother."

"Would it?"

"No." Her heartbeat kicked up a notch. "And we wouldn't have to pretend if we…"

He seemed to be waging an inner battle. Finally he stepped back. "No. I think you had the right idea in the first place."

She felt as if she'd been slapped. So he didn't trust her. So much for her barely formed hope that he might be in love with her. Apparently it was just sexual with him.

She crossed her arms once again. "Are you suggesting that maybe you should stay here all night on the couch and then invite her down for breakfast to prove that you were here? Because I don't think I could take that."

"Don't worry. Neither could I."

She was very disappointed. If only Jonah would pull her into his arms and declare that he trusted her not to tell her mother the intimate details. It didn't look as if he was going to do that. "So obviously you're not here to—"

"Seduce you? No."

He'd done a pretty fair job without even trying, she

thought. She took a deep breath and forced herself to think about the problem. Gradually she began to create a solution. "Excuse me a minute. I'll be right back."

She headed for the bedroom and opened a drawer in her desk. Her spare key was right where she kept it. As she picked it up, she wondered what it would be like if she were giving Jonah a key because they were lovers. She glanced at her bed, a walnut four-poster with a thick comforter and piles of pillows. If they were lovers, she would come home from a tough day on Wall Street and find Jonah lying there, waiting for her. Her body warmed at the fantasy.

Closing the drawer with a snap, she left the room before the strength of the fantasy pulled Jonah right in there with her. No telling what sort of pheromones she was giving out at the moment.

She walked back into the living room and found him crouched next to Bobo, who had rolled to his back to have his tummy scratched. Seeing them together like that reminded her that without Jonah's instinctive heroism, she might not have Bobo anymore. "Thank you," she said.

He glanced up. "For what?"

"Saving him. With all the confusion surrounding the bachelor auction and...our weekend together, I'm not sure I've really told you how much that means to me. I'm crazy about that dog, and if anything had happened to him, I hate to think the state I'd be in."

Jonah held her gaze. "I'm glad I happened to be there."

"Are you really? You've been hounded unmercifully ever since. I wondered if you ever regretted going in after him."

"No." He stood. "If any of my complaints made you

think I'd trade the life of your dog for getting my privacy back, I apologize. It was good for me to come down here tonight, if only to remind myself that your dog is alive and well. That's more important than dodging a few reporters."

"And your rescue gave my mother a topic for a book that seems to have cured her depression and maybe given her a career. The fact is that I have a lot to be grateful to you for."

He frowned. "Please tell me that's not why you went to bed with me."

She looked at him standing there in all his broad-shouldered glory, his shirt and jeans no barrier to her memory of what he'd looked like in his unclothed, aroused state. She almost laughed at his concern.

"No." She smiled at him. "And that's another thing I have to be grateful for."

14

JONAH ALMOST LOST the control he'd worked so hard to keep when Natalie smiled and told him she was grateful for the way he'd loved her. Somehow he stopped himself from crossing the room and hauling her into his arms. This little interview he was having with her really tested him. If he said he trusted her not to tell her mother everything, they'd be in her bedroom inside of five seconds. He could see it in her eyes.

In fact, he did trust her not to tell her mother everything. But he didn't trust her not to break his heart. So he'd decided on a course of action that would kill two birds with one stone. He'd set up some dates with Natalie and her mother. That would keep Alice from getting suspicious about their supposed love affair, and he would find out if he and Natalie had anything going for them besides sex.

Or gratitude. He didn't want a woman simply because she was grateful.

"Here's an extra key to my apartment." She walked over and held it out. "Maybe you'd like to move a few of your things over."

He stared at her. Talk about offering him a bite of the apple. "I thought we'd just agreed we weren't strong enough for that kind of game."

"I didn't mean that you'd actually stay here. But if a few of your things just happen to be around—some clothes, a toothbrush, a razor, then my mother will notice. If you can spare a bottle of your aftershave, I could spray it in the air every once in a while."

"Very creative." He took the key, the metal still warm from where she'd clutched it in her palm. Despite the way she'd described the arrangement, he couldn't help the leap of excitement in his veins just knowing he had access to her apartment anytime he wanted it. She was far more available to him than she'd been a minute ago.

She looked uneasy as he took out his keys and slid hers onto the ring. Maybe she regretted giving it to him, but it was done, and he pocketed the keys with a sense of potential.

"And for your information," she added, "I don't like pulling the wool over my mother's eyes any more than you do, but I don't see much choice."

"Neither do I."

"I thought if you had a key you could bring stuff over whenever you want. Some of your favorite beer in the refrigerator would be a nice touch."

"How about peanuts?" he asked quietly, just to get a reaction out of her. He would never be able to eat the damn things again without remembering that moment when he'd kissed her so thoroughly that she'd let the peanuts she'd been holding dribble onto the floor.

To his immense satisfaction, her cheeks bloomed pink. "Peanuts aren't necessary," she said.

He gazed at her a moment longer. If only he could be sure that her reaction to him was about more than sex. "So we have a game plan. Now we need to set up a date with you, me and your mother. When was the last time you spent Sunday afternoon at the art museum?"

"You mean the Met?"

"Okay, maybe that's too boring. I just realized it's so close that you probably go there all the time. I don't, and I thought—"

"No, no, I'd love to. I haven't been there in years. It would be fun."

"You'd really like to go?" He shouldn't put too much stock in her enthusiasm, he thought. Maybe she was only being nice. After all, what did they know about each other's interests?

"I would. And I'm sure my mother would. But aren't you worried about people recognizing us and causing a problem?"

"It's happening less and less every day. If something else newsworthy breaks soon, people will probably forget all about us."

"That would be a relief."

"It would be over by now if the bachelor auction hadn't reminded everybody who I was. Anyway, I think we can chance an afternoon at the Met. If your mom wants to go, I'll be here around one. Maybe we could grab some lunch at the—"

"Jonah, I don't want you spending a lot of money on this. We can eat before we go."

His jaw clenched. There she was, throwing the money issue in his face. Maybe she really did want to keep it as a barrier between them by continuing to remind him that he wasn't as financially well off as she was, even if it wasn't true. "I can afford to buy us lunch," he said. "And pay for the admission." He glanced at her. "Unless you want to set up an expense account I can draw from?"

"Now you're angry. I didn't mean to insult you. It's just that you've done so much already."

"You seem to forget that I had intended to ask you

out a long time ago. What did you suppose I'd have suggested for our first date, window-shopping and maybe a soft pretzel if I was feeling really flush? I'm not a pauper, Natalie." He gestured toward the windows fronting the street. "I don't happen to have that view, but I can afford a few lunches and museum tickets."

"Of course you can. I only—"

"Do you realize how patronizing you sound?"

"I don't mean to be! Jonah, you were sucked into this against your will, and you've behaved admirably under the circumstances. Now that I'm asking you to put up this front for my mother, is it so wrong for me to think about the money you'll have to spend?"

"It is when you know that I would enjoy doing it, that I—" He came to a screeching halt before he admitted things he had no intention of admitting at this stage in the game. God, his confidence was shot. At first he'd thought she was crazy about him, and now he was afraid he was only a necessary convenience who, luckily for her, happened to be a fair lover.

He could make her moan with delight in bed, but out of it she might just be tolerating his presence. He'd heard about women who kept men around because they were a sexual turn-on, but they never expected to have a real relationship with these boy toys. And Natalie certainly was keeping a lock on her secrets.

"I'm sorry." Her gray eyes were soft with regret. "You're trying to be a friend and I'm treating you like some sort of employee."

He'd love to ask her exactly what she thought of him, but he probably wouldn't get the truth, not when her mother still needed his help. No, she'd treat him the best she possibly could until Alice had what she needed. Until then, there was no point in having a showdown with her.

He sighed. "Apology accepted. I'll bring over the things you suggested sometime tomorrow while you're at work. That way we won't have to run into each other any more than necessary."

"Jonah, for what it's worth, I wish you had asked me out before that incident at the lake. I wish we had gotten to know each other under different circumstances."

"But once you start changing things, you have to realize everything would have changed, and your mother might not have thought to write a romance."

"I guess you're right."

"This is what we have, Natalie. We have to play it out and see where it takes us." He wished his heart didn't ache every time he looked into her eyes. He knew the look he wanted to see there, and it wasn't the one he was seeing. Right now she just looked harassed and confused. He walked over and picked up his coat from the couch before heading toward her front door. "Let me know about Sunday."

"I will."

With his hand on the doorknob, he glanced back at her. She looked forlorn and vulnerable as she stood alone, watching him leave. His natural instinct was to go back and take her in his arms. To hell with the consequences. He overrode that instinct.

"Good night," he said, and walked out the door.

JONAH SUFFERED the torture of the damned as he escorted Natalie and her mother all over town in the next few weeks. With every day he fell deeper in love, and he couldn't do a blessed thing about it until Alice's book was finished.

He made visits to Natalie's apartment every few days when she was at work and dropped off a different set of clothes and other pieces of evidence for her mother's benefit. The afternoon he brought over some beer he decided to drink one and leave it on the counter. Nice touch.

Nice touch, baloney. He was stalling, knowing that Natalie could walk in the door any minute and he could *accidentally* run into her. He was desperate to be alone with her for just a minute. Despite all the time they spent together, he missed her like the devil.

As he drank the beer, he wandered through the apartment, Bobo trailing along, while he soaked up the colors and textures of her world. Of course he ended up in her bedroom, running a hand over her pillow, picturing her lying there asleep. If only she dreamed of him. He even snooped in her closet and touched her clothes. He was fingering the material of the white blouse she'd worn on the yacht when Bobo raced for the front door.

As he emerged from the bedroom, she came through the door and closed it carefully behind her. "Dropping off a few things?" she said. Her voice sounded tight.

"Yeah." He hoisted the empty beer bottle. "I decided to leave an empty on the kitchen counter, for effect."

"But the kitchen's over there." She motioned toward the door across the room from where he stood.

"Just where I was headed." He walked toward the kitchen. God, but she affected him. And it wasn't all about sex, either. Not anymore. He would love to spend the evening just being here, watching her go about her chores. But he knew that eventually, if he hung around long enough, they'd end up in bed. As much as he wanted that, too, he didn't want to make love until they'd cleared the air, until he knew where he stood with her. Until Alice's book was finished.

"Would you...like to stay for dinner?" she called softly after him.

He almost groaned aloud. Of course he would. But he didn't dare. "Thanks, but I really have to be going," he said over his shoulder. He set the beer bottle down and came back into the living room. "So how's the book coming along?"

"I don't know." Her gaze was hungry as she looked at him.

"Do you think we're distracting her too much by taking her places? I could pretend to have some double shifts at work." He hated to cut down on their three-some dates, because then he'd hardly see Natalie at all, but if it meant the book would be done sooner, he'd force himself.

"No. She loves going out with us. I haven't seen her looking so happy in ages."

"Do you have any idea how far she is from the end?" He sounded desperate. Well, he *was* desperate.

"I've tried to find out. Once she said she was about three-quarters through, but the next time I asked, she'd gone back to rework all those chapters, so it's hard to say. Jonah, I—"

"What?" In that charged moment as he stared at her, he made a decision. If she asked him to love her, he'd do it. To hell with the plan.

"Never mind. I guess I'll see you tomorrow night for the play, huh?"

"Right." He grabbed his coat and started for the door. "See you then."

NATALIE FOUGHT THE URGE to run after him. If she begged him to make love to her and he refused because he didn't trust her, she wouldn't be able to stand it. She'd thought maybe they could at least sit and have dinner together, which would be better than nothing, but he'd rejected that proposal, so he probably would have rejected a more intimate one, too.

Bobo pranced around her, eager for his walk. "Okay, boy. In a minute." Slowly she walked into the kitchen and picked up the beer bottle he'd left on the counter. She cradled it in both hands, as if she could somehow absorb the warmth of his touch from the unyielding glass. Then she raised the bottle to her mouth and slowly ran the rim around her lips.

Closing her eyes, she concentrated on the memory of his kiss. Strangely enough, it wasn't the passion that she missed the most. She ached for the sense of connection, of not being alone in the world. Until Jonah, she hadn't known that feeling. Now she couldn't seem to live without it.

THROUGH THE TENSION-FILLED DAYS of missing Jonah, Natalie kept thinking of how she could thank him for helping her mother. She came up with the answer as she passed a sports memorabilia store when she was out for a walk on her lunch break. The perfect gift sat perched in the display window.

She was so excited about her purchase that she took it straight up to her mother's apartment when she got home that night.

Alice answered the door with a portion of her manuscript in one hand and her glasses perched on her nose.

"I'm not interrupting your writing, am I?" Natalie didn't want to slow the process one iota.

"No, I'm just going over the chapter I finished today. But I'm getting close to the end."

Natalie's pulse leaped. Soon. "That's great, Mom."

"What do you have there?"

Natalie shucked her coat and proudly took the gift out of the box. "Doesn't this just shout out *Jonah?*"

Alice put down her manuscript and stuck her pen behind her ear before she took the autographed basketball. "It shouts out *expensive*, that's for sure." She turned the ball around to examine all the signatures.

"They're all there." Natalie hugged herself with pleasure. "You know how he feels about the Knicks. I can hardly wait to see his face when I give him this."

"It's very nice, and I'm sure he'll love it. When is his birthday, anyway?"

"Uh...I didn't exactly buy it for his birthday." And she didn't even know when his birthday was, but she couldn't very well admit that to her mother. Any woman in love knew when her beloved was born.

"Surely you're not starting on Christmas already?"

"No, I just wanted to give him something because..." She couldn't tell Alice it was in gratitude for all Jonah had done, either. She probably shouldn't have brought the basketball up to show her mother in the first place, but she'd wanted to share her find with someone. "I wanted to give it to him because he's such a great guy, and I love him so much," she said.

Alice gave her daughter a sympathetic look. "I can understand that, sweetheart, but I'm not sure Jonah will."

"What do you mean?"

"Let's go sit down." Alice led the way into the living room and motioned Natalie to the couch. She positioned herself next to her daughter, the basketball cradled in her lap. "This cost a bundle, didn't it?"

"Well, sort of." Natalie had weathered sticker shock when she'd discovered what the shop was charging for the basketball, but it had been such a perfect gift that she'd bought it anyway.

"You used plastic, didn't you?"

Natalie could feel a lecture coming. "Okay, I know I've been throwing money around lately, but it's all in a good cause. Besides, things are looking up in the market these days, and I just landed a new client. I'll probably make some decent money this month."

Alice patted her daughter's folded hands. "I hope you do. And I'm sure you'll put the money back in your IRA eventually. You're very clever."

Natalie glanced down and noticed that she'd been twisting her hands in her lap. Not exactly a show of strength. Her mother knew she was whistling in the dark and that she'd have to work long and hard to replace that retirement money, but still Alice was giving her a vote of confidence.

"But that's not the point," Alice said. "The point is that Jonah knows you spent all that money to get him at the auction, and now on top of that, you're buying him this expensive gift, something more extravagant than he'd buy himself. I know you're doing all this because you have a very generous heart, sometimes too generous. But Jonah doesn't know you as well as I do, and I'm worried that he'll get the wrong idea."

Natalie's mouth felt dry. "You mean that I'm trying to buy his love?"

"Something like that. Or that you flaunt the fact that you have money. Have you told him yet that you sacrificed your retirement fund for the auction?"

"Not yet." And she wasn't looking forward to telling him, either. So far, she'd had no luck dealing with sensitive topics where Jonah was concerned. She always managed to present things in the wrong light.

"So he still thinks you're a wealthy young woman."

"I guess so."

"If I were you, I'd confess this whole business soon. Secrets like that put distance between two people, even when they're very much in love. I realize now I should have told your father about my writing."

Natalie glanced at her, startled. "But what if he'd been critical?"

"Then we would have gotten the matter out in the open. As it was, I cheated both of us. Don't let that happen to you, sweetheart. Tell him."

Natalie sighed. "I guess I should." But she cringed at the thought of letting Jonah know she'd misled him on yet another matter. Maybe she'd tell him soon, but not until after she'd given him the basketball. He would go nuts over it. Sure, he'd realize it was expensive, but that wasn't as significant as the fact she'd noticed his passion for the Knicks and had searched for something he would love to have. Surely that was more important than what she paid for the gift, wasn't it?

LESS THAN A WEEK LATER, Alice invited Natalie and Jonah to a celebration dinner. Although Alice wouldn't say what they were celebrating, Natalie was positive her mother had finished the first draft of her book.

Natalie hurried home from work to change into something more festive than her gray suit. Feeling like a spring flower spreading its petals after a long winter, she pulled a pink knit dress over her head and belted it with a multicolored sash. Her fingers shook as she wrapped the box containing the basketball. She'd invite Jonah to her apartment after dinner and give him the basketball.

And then…she didn't know what would happen, but she knew what she wanted to happen. She wanted the reserve to disappear from Jonah's manner. She wanted his passion to return and sweep her away, as it had all those long weeks ago. And she wanted him to tell her he loved her. Because she loved him with a depth that scared the dickens out of her, and if she didn't have a chance to tell him soon, she just might explode.

When she arrived at her mother's apartment Jonah was already there, a glass of his favorite beer on the end table as he sat on the couch reading what had to be a completed manuscript. From the stack of pages piled next to him, it looked as if he'd been there quite a while. Alice must have asked him to come early so he could read what she'd written.

Natalie was a little jealous that her mother had chosen Jonah as her first reader, but Jonah's input was the most important for the project. He started to put the manuscript aside as she came into the room.

"That's okay." She motioned him to continue. "Keep reading."

"Then I will, if you two don't mind. I'm almost finished."

"Can I get you anything?" Alice hovered around him like a nervous mother bird. "Another beer?"

"Nothing, thanks." Jonah seemed distracted as he returned immediately to the manuscript.

"Here's your copy, dear." Her mother handed Natalie a stack of pages tied with a red ribbon. "I'm sure you guessed what this little dinner was all about."

"I did." Natalie took the manuscript and gave her mother a big hug. "Congratulations, Mom."

"I'm a wreck," Alice whispered to her. "Come on in the kitchen where we won't bother Jonah. Would you like a glass of wine? I think I'll have one. I think I'll have six."

"Hey, I'm sure it's great." A protective arm around her mother's waist, Natalie walked with her back to the kitchen filled with the aroma of roast beef. "I still remember the first three chapters of the one you wrote before. I loved them."

"Yes, and you were twelve years old and my daughter. You were probably amazed that I could write fiction at all. It's like the dancing bear. He doesn't do it well, but you're impressed he can do it at all." Alice took a bottle of their favorite Chardonnay out of the refrigerator and rummaged for the corkscrew in a kitchen drawer.

"I was brilliant at twelve," Natalie said, grinning at her mother. "I was reading the classics by then. I would have recognized dreck if I'd seen it. Your story was good." She took two glasses from the cupboard. "I'll bet this one is even better."

Alice pried the cork from the bottle and poured the glasses full. "It could be donkey dung. I can't tell. But at least I finished it. At least I don't have to say, 'Someday I'll write a book' anymore."

"Darn right." Natalie picked up her wineglass and lifted it. "To living your dreams."

Her mother picked up her glass and clinked it softly with Natalie's. Her eyes were moist. "That's exactly what this feels like." She looked squarely at Natalie. "Thank you."

15

JONAH FINISHED Alice's book and sat with the final page in his hand while he absorbed what he'd read. The story was funny, passionate and technically accurate. Alice had paid close attention to everything he had told her about the business of fighting fires.

But he couldn't find any trace of himself in the hero. She'd made him blond, for one thing, and shorter. Bobo's rescue was transformed—the hero saved a kitten from an electrical pole and possible electrocution on a loose wire. She hadn't used the bachelor auction at all, which would have been a dead giveaway. And the love scenes were hot, but he didn't recognize anything about them other than the obvious similarities when any couple had sex.

The book was about a firefighter who meets a woman because he saves her pet, but other than that, the story bore no resemblance to Jonah's life. He was incredibly relieved, but he wondered what she'd done with all that research into his childhood. This guy was an orphan, which Alice had used as part of the plot complication as he searched for his lost parents. The book's hero was a loner afraid to commit, while Jonah had so many people in his life he had trouble keeping track of them all, and as for commitment, he was ready. Natalie was the iffy part of the equation.

Stacking the pages carefully and tapping them into a

neat bundle, he set the manuscript on the coffee table, picked up his beer glass and stood. Then he stretched and glanced at his watch. Amazing. He'd sat there for almost three hours reading a romance. Although he was no judge of such things, he thought Alice's book should be published.

And now…his contribution was finished. Natalie's reason for bidding on him at the auction had been satisfied. She had no more reason to string him along.

Maybe she'd want to keep having sex with him now that her mother's book was finished, but he had no idea if she wanted more than that. Perhaps it wasn't a fair test, but he thought it all turned on whether she'd tell him about spending her retirement money. If she could be that vulnerable and let him know she wasn't rich and she was also a little foolish, then maybe she wanted more than his presence in her bed.

If she couldn't or wouldn't tell him, then he didn't hold out much hope for them.

He walked into the kitchen where Natalie and her mother were gathered in front of the open oven door peering at a standing rib roast that looked delicious. Now that Jonah knew Alice wasn't wealthy, he was touched that she'd bought such an expensive cut of meat for this celebration.

The minute Alice realized he was there she slammed the oven door and whirled to face him, her face taut with dread.

"It's great," he said, so glad he could say that honestly. He'd wondered what he'd do if the book had turned out to be awful. "I don't even read romances, but I couldn't put it down."

"Oh!" Alice ran across the kitchen and grabbed him in a bear hug, causing him to slop his beer on the floor.

She didn't seem to notice as she thanked him profusely over and over while she continued to hug him. He hugged her back with his free arm while he looked across the room at Natalie.

She had a big smile on her face, but when he looked into her eyes he could see the tears gathered there. He'd sure love to know what they meant. They might be tears of joy. Or they might be tears of regret that now she'd have to face the consequences of what she'd done for her mother. Maybe she didn't want this inconvenient firefighter hanging around now that his usefulness had ended, and she had no idea how to gracefully get rid of him.

If that turned out to be the case, he wouldn't make it difficult for her.

Alice finally released him and stepped back to take a deep breath and wipe her eyes. "Thank you, Jonah, both for your help and for liking the book."

"Neither one was hard to do," he said. "But I do have a question."

Alice looked apprehensive again. "I botched the fire scene, didn't I? I wondered if I got it right, so if there's anything wrong, I'll fix it right up. That's one reason I wanted you to—"

"Nothing's wrong with the fire scene. You got everything right. The guys at the station will love reading it when it's published."

"You really think it will be?"

"It has my vote."

"Oh, my." Alice drew another shaky breath. "I hope Heart Books agrees with you."

"So do I. But I wondered about the hero. Why did you ask me all those questions about my childhood when the hero's an orphan?"

Alice looked guilty. "You'll have to forgive me. My only defense is that I'm a mother. I wanted to find out your background so that I'd know more about the man my daughter has fallen in love with. The book research was a perfect excuse to snoop, and I took it. I hope you don't mind."

Jonah glanced at Natalie to see how she was taking this. Her expression had become more guarded and his stomach clenched. "No, I don't mind," he said to Alice.

"I thought it was an even exchange, considering all the family stories I told you so you'd know Natalie a little better."

"Yeah, I appreciate that." He flashed a grin at Natalie because he figured Alice expected him to. He was not encouraged by the weak smile he got in return or the wariness in her eyes.

"What I'm dying to know," Alice said, "is whether you two have started making plans. After all, you've been constantly together for weeks, so you must be thinking about making it official. My guess is that you wanted to hold off telling me until I finished my project, and you're afraid you'll steal my thunder by announcing anything tonight. But you'd do nothing of the kind." She glanced up with affection at Jonah. "I'd love to celebrate both things at once. So tell me, am I about to get a son-in-law?"

NATALIE'S HOPES died as she saw the trapped look on Jonah's face. He was no more ready to commit to her than don a cape and fly over Manhattan. Yet it wasn't surprising that her mother would ask such a question. After all, they'd put on a wonderful show of being madly in love. They'd obviously done too good a job, and now Alice expected a wedding.

As Jonah fumbled for an answer, Natalie rushed to his aid. "We still have a lot of things to settle before we do that, Mom," she said. "And besides, I know Jonah wants me to meet his family. We've both been too busy to even think about a trip to Buffalo, but we don't want to set a date before we do that, right, sweetheart?"

"That's right." Jonah met her gaze. "My folks would kill me if I announced I was getting married and they hadn't even met my bride-to-be."

"Oh." Alice seemed to sag as all her former excitement drained away. "Well, of course. How self-centered of me. I completely forgot that you'd want to bring your parents into this before you announced anything." She glanced around as if searching for a change of subject. "Goodness, I didn't notice that I'd made you spill your beer. Let's clean it up and then we'll eat. Everything's ready."

"I'll clean it up," Jonah said. "Just give me a sponge."

The two of them began to bustle around the kitchen, but Natalie couldn't seem to move. She was immobilized by the picture of her mother a moment ago, and how the starch had gone right out of her once she discovered there were no wedding plans to celebrate. For a few seconds her posture was disturbingly similar to the old Alice, the one who had disappeared soon after Jonah rescued Bobo.

A horrible possibility occurred to Natalie. What if it wasn't just the creation of the book that had lifted her mother's depression? What if her good spirits were also tied to this romance her daughter was having with Jonah and the promise of an impending wedding?

The idea haunted Natalie throughout the meal. Vaguely she realized that both Jonah and her mother kept giving her strange looks. Every time she was aware they were doing it, she made a conscious effort to join in the conversation. Most of the talk centered around Alice's next step and whether she should contact an agent or just send the manuscript straight to the publisher.

"In a way, it'll be hard to let it go," Alice said. "I've loved working on it. When I go into that fantasy world, I forget about my own problems."

"Won't you start another book right away?" Natalie asked. She'd never thought beyond the completion of this one. Now she worried that her mother would sit around waiting to hear whether this one sold. If it didn't, that might put her right back where she'd been before, crying and working picture puzzles. Natalie panicked at the thought. "It's probably a good idea to plunge right into the next project so you won't be obsessing about what the editor will decide," she said.

"I suppose you're right," her mother agreed. "But I've been so caught up in these characters, I can't imagine thinking up new ones right now."

Natalie figured desperation was her only excuse for what came out of her mouth next. "I know just the person you should talk with. His name's Pete, and he lives in Jonah's apartment building. He has an absolutely wonderful imagination, and I'll bet he'd love to brainstorm story ideas with you."

Jonah looked at her as if she'd lost her mind. "How do you know Pete has a good imagination?" he asked.

"I talked with him a couple of different times, and it was pretty obvious. I even found out he makes up stories to tell his grandchildren." She risked a glance at her mother, who was staring at her.

"Natalie," Alice said slowly, "you wouldn't be trying to fix me up, now, would you?"

"Of course not!" Natalie could feel the blush rising to her cheeks. In a way that was exactly what she was doing. She was beginning to realize that she couldn't handle her mother's situation all by herself, and she didn't know the people in her building well enough to enlist them on short notice. Ironically, she knew the people in Jonah's building better than the ones in her own, and Pete might be just the ticket. "But I think you'd like him." She sent a pleading glance toward Jonah. "Wouldn't it be fun if the four of us took in a movie sometime?"

"Um, sure. We could do that."

"We'll do nothing of the kind," Alice said. "You *are* trying to fix me up, and I won't have it."

Jonah put down his fork and turned to face her. "Okay, I'll admit it. Natalie and I thought you two would hit it off, but we weren't sure how to bring up the subject. Natalie caught me by surprise, mentioning it now, but it's probably the perfect time. I can vouch for Pete. I've known him for five years and he's a terrific guy. He's been widowed ever since I've known him and seems to be getting along okay, but I think he's probably lonely. Natalie's right. He'd love talking about story ideas with you."

Natalie longed to hug the breath out of him for that. She sent him a grateful smile.

"So the two of you have been conniving, have you?" Alice seemed pleased with the idea. "Well, I'm not interested in a date, really, but I suppose a foursome would be fun. I sometimes feel like a fifth wheel when I go out with you, although I've loved every minute and couldn't force myself to turn down any of your invitations."

Natalie's heart clutched at her mother's vulnerability. "We loved having you go along, didn't we, Jonah?"

"Absolutely. It's been a great few weeks."

The way he said it sounded almost as if they'd come to the end of an era, and Natalie couldn't shake off that feeling herself. But Jonah was nothing if not kind. He wouldn't abruptly abandon her mother to her own devices, even if he wanted to break off with Natalie. Just from the way he'd supported her suggestion tonight, she knew that he'd be happy to help introduce Alice to Pete and nurture that friendship before he bowed out of the picture.

The prospect of an outing with Pete seemed to perk Alice up considerably, as if it was a guarantee that her social life wouldn't end with the last chapter of her book. She served a pudding laced with rum and set it on fire with the flair that Natalie remembered from the days when her father had been alive. Natalie gave silent thanks that another hurdle seemed to have been crossed.

Inevitably, however, the evening came to an end. Natalie knew her mother expected Jonah to spend the night in her apartment as they'd implied he'd done many times before. Earlier in the day, she'd wondered if that might actually happen this time, but now she wasn't so sure. Jonah might be ready to get rid of these two women who had turned his life inside out.

With her copy of the manuscript under her arm, Natalie gave her mother a hug as she stood with Jonah in the entry hall. "Congratulations, again, Mom. You did it."

"Let's hope it sells," Alice said. "But I am pleased with myself for getting this far. A few months ago I wouldn't have thought I could manage it." She drew back and included Jonah in her smile. "Thanks to both of you, I was inspired."

"Yeah, but you did the work." Jonah gave her a hug, too.

Natalie found herself getting misty-eyed again as she watched her mother and Jonah embrace. They'd obviously formed a close relationship and now there was no telling what would happen with that. If Natalie had been able to keep her feelings for Jonah on a friendship level, the three of them could have maintained their connection indefinitely. But she couldn't be just friends with Jonah—not anymore.

"I'll talk to Pete about getting together soon," Jonah said as he released Alice and started toward the door.

A light flush tinged Alice's cheeks. "Not that it's important, of course, but is he...attractive?"

Jonah grinned. "Better-looking than me."

"Now, that's impossible. Good night, you two. You've been great company, as usual." Alice smiled at them, waved and closed the door.

Natalie glanced up at Jonah. "Well, that's that."

His expression gave nothing away. "Guess so."

She realized he wasn't going to give her any help. At least she'd present him with the autographed basketball, she decided. "If you'd like to come to my place for a minute, I have something for you."

His eyebrows lifted.

"It's something I saw and thought of you. It's—well, you'll just have to see."

"Okay."

They walked to the elevator and rode down in silence. Natalie kept sneaking glances at him, but he gave no indication of what he might be thinking.

Belatedly Natalie remembered she had a couple of specific things to thank him for. "It was wonderful the way you complimented Mom on her book," she said as the elevator opened and they started toward her apartment.

"I meant what I said. It's a good story."

"I'm sure it is. But the way you said what you did, telling her with that intense look in your eyes that it was great—I'm sure she felt very special at that moment."

"And what intense look would that be?"

"You know. The one where your eyes get all dark and the person knows they have your complete attention. It's very...validating."

"Hmm." He had his key out before she'd reached in the pocket of her dress for hers. He unlocked the door with practiced ease.

The familiar way he walked into her apartment stirred the first embers of desire within her. He'd wanted her once. She wondered if he wanted her still.

Bobo greeted each of them with equal enthusiasm. From the way Jonah talked to the dog and gave him a thorough head-to-tail petting, Natalie suspected he'd spent time playing with the dog every time he'd come over to exchange the clothes they'd been using as props. She was completely absorbed in the homey picture of man and dog together. How she wanted to make the image hold.

He gave Bobo a final pat and straightened. "You said you had something for me?"

With only one lamp on in the living room she had trouble seeing the expression in his eyes. Maybe the shadows were playing tricks on her, but she imagined a light of excitement there. Perhaps there was hope for them.

"I'll get it." She went into the bedroom to retrieve the gift-wrapped box she'd left on the dresser.

As she picked it up, she heard the bedroom door click softly closed. She turned to find him standing just inside the room, gazing at her. She looked into his eyes and didn't miss the message in them this time.

Her heartbeat went crazy. "I...I didn't get a card. Nothing seemed appropriate." She sounded like an idiot, but she couldn't just tell him to forget the damn present and take her, instead. She soldiered on. "I just thought, after all you've been through because of me and all the help you've given my mother, that you deserved something in return."

"I see." His gaze held the intensity she'd described minutes ago.

She'd told him that look was validating—a socially acceptable word she'd decided to use at the time because she'd hesitated to be more explicit. But that gaze was more...so much more. When he looked at her with that dark fire in his eyes, a circuit connected that sent pulses of energy to every part of her body. At first the pulses only warmed, but then the heat started, until she was blazing and breathless, longing to burn.

He took the box. She wondered if he'd set it aside and pull her into his arms, but instead he ripped the wrapping off. The display box allowed him to see what was inside through a plastic window, and his eyes widened. He opened the box and dropped it and the wrapping paper to the floor as he turned the basketball slowly, rubbing his finger over the signatures.

Finally he glanced at Natalie. "These are damn expensive."

"It doesn't matter. The point is that you—"

His voice was dangerously soft. "The point is that you can afford it, right?"

She stood, wrapped with indecision. How could she confess that she was broke while he was holding a gift she'd bought on credit? She could see how special the basketball was to him, but if he thought she couldn't afford it, he'd make her take it back. The gesture would be ruined.

"I can afford it," she said.

His expression hardened. "You're sure about that?"

"Yes."

He muttered an oath under his breath.

"What's wrong? I can tell you like the basketball."

"Of course I like the basketball." His fingers tightened on it. "You knew I would."

"Then what is it?"

"Nothing." He turned the basketball in his hands and seemed to force a smile. "It's great, Natalie. Thanks."

Her heart broke. The extravagant gift had embarrassed him, weighed him down with obligations he didn't want. He might need her sexually, but his plans for her didn't extend beyond that.

Well, if all he wanted was sex from her, she'd ignore the weeping in her heart and give herself to him. It would be an act of love, but he would never know. Perhaps the strength of her love would be enough to carry her through the realization that for him, it was just a physical act.

She loosened the sash around her waist. "The book's done, Jonah," she murmured.

SO THAT WOULD BE the way of it, he thought as pain engulfed him. She would buy him off with an expensive gift. Sure, she wanted him to make love to her, but she didn't want him to be in love with her. Unfortunately, he couldn't help it. Still, if the meeting of their bodies was all she wanted, he would give her the best he had to offer.

"Yes, the book's done." He rolled the basketball gently across the bed and it bounced softly on the carpet on the far side. "I've missed you." He drew her into his arms. So sweet. If only she could feel the same love beating through her veins that throbbed in his.

"I've missed you, too." She closed her eyes and lifted her face for his kiss.

He spared a moment to gaze at her, cherishing the tilt of her nose and the curve of her cheek. He would love her tonight, but after that he might have to beg off to keep himself from coming apart. As pleasure and despair spun dizzily through him, he leaned down and slowly tasted the lips that had been denied him for so long.

Her moan of delight nearly broke him. He wanted the right to make her moan like that for the rest of her life. Realizing that some other man would have that privilege brought on violent emotions that had no place in this bedroom tonight. He pushed the thought aside and deepened the kiss.

She responded, but then she always had. The chemistry between them had been incredible from the beginning. But as he undressed her, it was more than chemistry guiding his hands. Each touch, each caress carried the love he couldn't say aloud. She might put the perfection of their mating down to technique, but when he was loving Natalie, he didn't even have to think. Instinct took over.

She fumbled with his clothes and he took some satisfaction in her eagerness. She might not love him, but she wanted him more than any woman he'd ever been with. By the time he lowered her to the bed she was trembling and gasping with the force of her need.

And he was no more controlled than she was. His erection throbbed as he quivered with the desire to push deep and claim her. But this might be the last time he'd ever know that moment, the last time he'd ever kiss her breasts, her thighs, all the secret places he'd enjoyed those long weeks ago. So he took his time, and she grew wild.

He liked making her wild. He wanted her to remember tonight for the rest of her life, even if she didn't plan to spend that lifetime with him. Finally the red haze of passion blotted out all reason. He sheathed himself and moved between her thighs, unable to hold back any longer.

As he gazed down at her, she opened her eyes. The fire there was real, and something else glimmered in those gray eyes, something…something tender and… but no, he must be mistaken. And he didn't dare make that mistake. With a groan of surrender, he slid into paradise for the last time.

NATALIE TRIED to quell the rising tide of her climax. As much as her body clamored for release, she didn't want the moment to end. For this night of lovemaking was goodbye. She couldn't put herself through this again.

But Jonah knew her too well. His steady movements carried her relentlessly to the brink and quickly hurled her over it with a glorious fury that brought tears to her eyes and a cry to her lips. But a last shred of self-preservation kept her from crying out the words that beat against her heart.

Jonah followed soon after, his own groan of satisfaction seeming to come from deep within his heart.

For one shining moment Natalie wondered if...but no, that was only fantasy. Still, she snuggled against him, needing to be stroked, needing to be cuddled, needing to keep him there a little longer.

Instead, he left the bed, and in no time he was dressing again.

She tried to steel herself, but it wasn't working. "Do you...have to go right away?" she asked in a tremulous voice.

"Yes."

"I thought maybe—"

He avoided her gaze. "I have to, Natalie. I wish I could stay. I wish I could be the person you want, a good-time guy to have around, no strings attached, but that's not me. And so I have to go. I'll be in touch." He opened the bedroom door, said something to Bobo and started out of the apartment.

No strings attached? In her dazed state it took Natalie a few seconds to register what he'd said. Once she had, she bolted from the bed and threw on her clothes. Then she grabbed the basketball and ran into the hall. She didn't realize she'd left the door open until Bobo bounded after her, barking with joy. She didn't dare stop to take him back.

"Jonah!"

He turned, his finger on the elevator button.

"Don't you dare get in that elevator!"

Bobo barked with even more excitement, as if he really liked this game, and an apartment door opened down the hall as the tenant peeked out to see what was going on.

"You forgot your basketball," Natalie said breathlessly as she reached Jonah.

He glanced down at the basketball but made no move to take it.

She swallowed the lump of nervousness in her throat. Maybe she'd misunderstood what he'd said a moment ago. Maybe she was about to make a complete fool of herself. She pressed the basketball against her fluttering stomach. "Who says I don't want strings?" she asked.

He looked startled.

She took a shaky breath and found the courage to look into his dark eyes. "Maybe I'm crazy about strings."

His jaw tightened and he glanced at the basketball again. "You could have fooled me. That's a kiss-off gift if I ever saw one."

"It is not a kiss-off gift!"

"No?"

"No!" Another door opened a crack and curious eyes peered at them. Natalie ignored them. "I bought it because I wanted you to have something special, because I know how much you love the Knicks and to show you how much I—"

"To show me how much money you had, you mean!" His eyes blazed. *"I can afford it, Jonah. Don't spend too much money on me, but I can afford to spend a lot on you, because I have it to spare."*

Heat washed over her as she understood. What an idiot she'd been not to tell him sooner. "I don't have a lot of money," she said. "In fact, I blew my retirement fund to buy you at the auction. I put this basketball on credit, but I'd do it again. I'd do it all again! I don't care about the money!"

By now doors were open all up and down the hall and a few neighbors had come out to stand and watch, as if she and Jonah were an interesting street act. She had no time to worry about them as she gazed at Jonah, waiting for him to explode at the idea that she'd been so foolish as to spend her retirement money on him. To her amazement, he began to smile.

"Okay, so I'm a financial disaster," she said. "Go ahead and laugh. I'm completely broke and I can't afford this basketball, but I'm not returning it to the store, and that's final."

"Oh, I wouldn't want you to return it." A soft light came into his eyes. "But I would like to know exactly why you bought it, considering it's totally out of your price range."

"I wanted you to have it."

"Not good enough. Why did you want me to have it?"

"Because…" She became aware of all the neighbors standing in the hallway, and suddenly she longed for a bit more privacy.

"Because why?" Jonah prompted.

To hell with it, she thought. Privacy was highly overrated, anyway. "Because I love you!" She glanced around at the neighbors as if daring them to comment.

"Hey, that's great." Jonah took her by the shoulders. "Because I love you, too."

Natalie stared up at Jonah, her heart pounding as a big smile bloomed on his face. "You do?"

"I do. And I'm prepared to repeat that in front of the

first available preacher, if you'll stand there and say it with me."

All the happiness in the world seemed gathered in this narrow hallway as she gazed at the man she loved. "Yes. Yes, a thousand times, yes."

Jonah's eyes glowed. "Looks like we need a trip to Buffalo."

"Looks like."

A smattering of applause soon turned into a resounding ovation as the neighbors voiced their approval. "String city!" called out one of the neighbors.

Jonah glanced around at the onlookers and back at Natalie. "Do you know your neighbors well?"

"No, but I have a feeling that's about to change."

He grinned. "I guess that rules out the idea of a small wedding."

Natalie began to laugh. "You actually thought that the wedding of the sexy fireman and his puppy lady would be small?"

Jonah groaned. "Here we go again."

"And you're going to love every minute."

"I'm going to love you every minute." He gave her a quick, hard kiss. "I'll tolerate all the trappings. Come on." He wrapped an arm around her shoulders and led her down the hall as Bobo pranced happily around them. "Let's go home." As he walked past the smiling neighbors, he nodded to each of them. "I'm Jonah Hayes, folks," he said. "I'm sure we'll all be seeing a lot more of each other in the future."

"Not the direction..."

He stilled. Slowly he lifted his head to look into her grey eyes, brimming with sunshine. "She didn't?"

"She wanted to talk... How soon did you say Mrs. R. would get here?" she said, mischief in her present.

Epilogue

ON HIS WAY DOWN the hall, Jonah called out a greeting to Mrs. Heinrich, the sweet little lady who lived on Natalie's floor. A month ago he'd helped her paint her bathroom, and he and Natalie had been enjoying Mrs. Heinrich's apple strudel ever since. Between the strudel and the zabaglione Mrs. R. brought over every time she visited, Jonah had been forced to increase his jogging sessions. Good thing he lived right next to the park now.

As he fit his key in the lock, he experienced the familiar tug of homecoming that would never grow old. He loved being married, loved making a cozy home, and more than either of those things, he loved Natalie LeBlanc Hayes.

She flung open the door before he could turn the knob. "Look! The first copies of Mom's book!"

"Really?" He grabbed her with one arm and took the book in his free hand. Kicking the door shut with his foot, he ignored Bobo temporarily while he indulged himself in a long, luxurious kiss.

"The book," Natalie murmured when he came up for air.

"Right. The book." He started to return to her full lips.

She put her fingertips over his mouth. "I think you'd better take a look."

"I will. But I've already read it."

"Not the dedication."

He stilled. Slowly he lifted his head to look into soft gray eyes brimming with laughter. "She didn't."

"She wanted to acknowledge all you did for her." Natalie looked as if she would burst into giggles at any moment.

"Aw, hell." Jonah released her, opened the paperback in his hand and turned to the dedication page. *To firefighter and hero Jonah Hayes, for making this book possible.* He glared at Natalie. "Did you know about this?"

"I didn't. I swear." She grinned. "I bet Pete will be jealous."

He rubbed a hand over his face. "Oh, boy. That's all I need. How many people buy these?"

"In this country?"

He stared at her in horror. "It goes to *other* countries?"

"Of course. Heart Books has a very wide distribution."

"*Natalie.*"

"Oh, relax." She patted his cheek. "Being an international hero isn't such a bad thing. Think of what it will do for your image with your kid."

"I don't have a kid." He gazed at her as she continued to smile. Oh, God. She'd mentioned a doctor's appointment today, but he'd thought it was routine. His vocal cords refused to work. "Do I?" he croaked.

"You have a start on one. Maybe even two."

He stood there as a warm feeling poured over him like syrup. "Yeah?"

"Yeah. You're gonna be a daddy at last."

"Hot damn." He scooped her up and whirled her around while she laughed and called him crazy. Bobo scampered in their wake, barking shrilly. Finally he set her down and bracketed her face with both hands. He'd imagined what it would be like to love a woman this much, but his imagination hadn't done the feeling justice. "I love you."

The look in her eyes fed all his fantasies. "And I love you," she murmured. Then her lips curved in an elfin smile and her voice deepened to a sexy whisper. "You're my hero."

"You know, when you say it like that..." He leaned down, his lips a fraction from hers. "It doesn't sound half-bad." Then he settled in to enjoy a hero's reward.

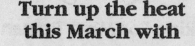

COMING NEXT MONTH

#725 JUST FOR THE NIGHT Leandra Logan
Bachelor Auction

Shari Johnson had spent her *entire* inheritance bidding on Garrett McNamara! Secretly she fantasized about the gorgeous bachelor and wanted him "just for the night." No strings. After all, she ran a coffee shop...and he was a millionaire. But Shari hadn't counted on him wanting her every night—forever.

#726 SAY "AHHH..." Donna Sterling
Bedside Manners, Book 1

Dr. Connor Wade thought he had a pretty good bedside manner...until his newest patient, Sarah Flowers, almost ran from his office at the mere sight of him. But Sarah had her reasons. She'd been expecting old Doc Bronkowski, and no way was she going to bare her soul—or anything else—to Dr. Tall Dark 'n' Handsome!

#727 TANGLED SHEETS Jo Leigh
The Wrong Bed

Maggie Beaumont was determined to seduce her fiancé, Gary, at the masquerade party. But somehow in the dark she ended up in the arms of the *wrong* man! Or was Spencer really Mr. Right? He was sexy, loving—and determined to have Maggie to himself.

#728 BREATHLESS Kimberly Raye
Blaze

Ten years ago, Tack Brandon hightailed it out of Inspiration, Texas, leaving behind his home, his family—and the girl he'd made a woman. Now he's back—and Annie Divine wants to get even. Following Tack's example, she planned to love him within an inch of his life...and then walk away. If only his kisses didn't leave her breathless....